THE GAME WAS JOINED

Elizabeth Brown had a piece of paper in her possession that could strip the Marquis of Montreat of his title, estates and social position should she deign to make it public.

For his part, the Marquis had the power to make Elizabeth tremble at his touch and quiver at his kisses, despite her passionate pride and most firm resolve.

Obviously they each had strong suits to play in this game of danger, deceit, intrigue and romance.

The question was, who would win—this Lord who would not back down, or this young lady who would not give in . . . ?

My Lord Rakehell

Margaret SeBastian

POPULAR LIBRARY • NEW YORK

POPULAR LIBRARY EDITION
April, 1977

ISBN: 0-445-03211-1

He walked in and came to a stop, just beyond the little entrance way of the shop, and struck a pose: the very picture of prideful arrogance.

He stood stiffly erect, one foot placed slightly forward, his two hands clasping his ivory-topped walking stick closely to his chest, his elbows turned outward.

He was dressed in the highest style of fashion as executed by the best of tailors as to cut but, as to color, his black coat hanging open revealed his black waistcoat and black small clothes, all serving to stress the white of his lace-edged cravat and the white of the lace at his wrists. One would hesitate to say his appearance was in the best of taste but, in any group of gentlemen of fashion, he must stand out as must a blot of ink upon a silken rainbow.

Slowly his gaze wandered over the shop and she rose to her feet from behind the little table where she had been doing the accounts. His only acknowledgment that he was aware of her presence was to remove his hat, a courtesy rarely observed by the usual sort of gentlemen to be encountered in her establishment.

He stepped over to the shelf-lined wall and, resting upon his stick, he brought his quizzing glass up to his eye and began to survey the titles of the volumes displayed on the shelves.

"May I be of service, sir?" she asked.

"No, you may not!" he replied abruptly. Rather coldly, she thought. "This is the shop of one Charles Brown?"

"Yes, it is, sir, but—"

"You may give him my compliments. I see he has an excellent collection."

"Thank you, sir, but—"

"Mr. Brown has been recommended to me as one who is expert in the sphere of books and documents. I am pleased to see that the contents of his shelves speak well of him."

He reached into his waistcoat and produced a card. Negligently he held it out to her. "You will inform Mr. Brown that I have a wish to speak to him on a matter of business."

Since he remained unmoving, she perforce must approach him to receive the card. She might have expected such lofty airs from some of her patronesses, but it was most unpleasant to discover them in a patron; since, without exception, her customers were scholars or professional men of serious bent and acceptable courtesy. She glanced at the card and, at once, sank into a low curtsy.

"Your lordship, I am honored that you deign to visit my humble shop," she said.

For the first time, he brought his gaze full upon her. There was the slightest hint of a frown on his forehead and one eyebrow lifted. He saw, easily, that the tight little smile upon her lips confirmed the mock humility in her voice.

"You are an insolent wench—or ignorant! I shall assume the latter and inform you that you overdo your genuflection. I am not of the blood royal."

"Quite!" she said as she arose.

"So it *is* insolence! Your master shall hear of this! Now get you gone, at once, and bring him to me!"

"Your lordship is speaking to the proprietor. I have this shop from my father who is deceased these past four years."

"You have my sympathy," he said coldly, "but most assuredly you shall not have my custom!" And he turned on his heels and strode towards the door.

"I am disconsolate, your lordship," she said.

Upon that, he wheeled about and glared at her. She returned his look and her chin rose defiantly. He walked purposefully back to her.

"Mrs. Brown—I am sure so you must be styled if this is a sample of how you deal—"

She broke in upon him flushing. "Thank you for

the compliment, your lordship. It is of a character that goes with the rest of your demeanor."

He remained staring at her, fingering his cane. He did not see anything particularly remarkable. She was of no great beauty, one might even have considered her plain but that her eyes were unusually piercing and that she stood before him as though they were equals.

"You are a most unusual female," he remarked. "You puzzle me greatly. Before I leave, will you be kind enough to inform me why you have taken me in such dislike? Of course, except that I am curious, it is no great matter, you will understand."

"Of course and I do. Therefore, I would not bore you. Good day, your lordship."

He did not budge, but studied her carefully as he demanded: "*You* dare dismiss *me?*"

"I beg your pardon, your lordship, but you misunderstood," she demurred, respectfully. "You may stay and browse as long as you wish. I only thought that our conversation was at an end."

"You have not answered my question."

"I thought I had."

"I mean in regard to your distaste for me."

"You said it was of no consequence."

"I have changed my mind."

Now it was her turn to study him. He was smiling at her, but it was a crooked smile and she did not doubt he was sneering at her.

"Your lordship, the name and fame of the Marquis of Montreat has penetrated even to this back street."

He laughed. "Are all your customers white angels? You cannot have many if they are."

"I do not know. I do not inquire into their behavior and am not so concerned so long as they treat me with the respect due a gentlewoman."

"Ah! I see! I have not, and so you must needs throw my ill repute in my face. Do you realize that if you were a man, I should horsewhip you?"

"If I were a man, your lordship, you would have behaved with greater reserve; but, as it is women you prey upon and I am a woman, your conduct comes as no great surprise. And I will, by your leave, point out to you that the color—or lack of it—that you affect in your dress is most appropriate."

"Why do I stand here listening to you!" he exclaimed, irritated. "How dare you judge me? You condemn me as a blackhearted villain out of hand. You do not know me! The tattle of gossiping crones and the odiois tripe served up in the penny dreadfuls fills your head, and with such evidence you build your case against me. I pray you will allow *me* to plead my cause!"

She blinked in surprise. "My lord marquis, I-I-this is most unseemly in you. Surely you do not have to convince me, a mere shopkeeper, of anything at all."

His white teeth flashed in a most engaging grin, and she experienced a strange emotion, not in the least unpleasant. It was quickly followed by a strong sense of danger.

He said winningly: "But surely then it must speak to some good purpose in me that I am concerned with your opinion of me."

Now she understood the panic that was beginning to mount in her breast. "I see your game, my lord. You are a most charming gentleman and have a way with you. You will not be withstood even by such as I. Very well, I will admit that I am not untouched. Will that satisfy you? Or must you conquer me completely as you have so many others, to feed your overweening pride?"

The smile disappeared from his face, and he looked very much discomfited.

"Does the shoe fit too snugly, my lord?" she inquired softly.

He looked hard at her as though he were trying to penetrate to the innermost recesses of her mind.

"You are Mrs. Brown." It was really a question.

"I am not as old as that! It will be years, I hope, before I am beyond the style of Miss Brown."

"Why *are* you not wed?"

"With all due respect, your lordship, that is *my* business."

He tapped his cane idly upon the floor. "I believe that you and I would do well together."

"You do not give up easily, your lordship."

"I am quite serious, Miss Brown."

"I do not doubt it, your lordship."

"I want you, Miss Brown."

She laughed and there was a bitter note to her laughter. "All I have is my reputation and this little shop. You would deprive me of both."

"It would be well worth your while."

"I do not doubt that it would for the little time it would take for you to completely captivate me. Then, what is to become of me after you have had your fill? Would you pass me on to some bosom beau?"

"That will be up to you. I will make a settlement on you so that you will never be in need no matter how things turn out."

"My lord, your generosity is only outdone by your salaciousness. If you are willing to go so far to satisfy your sensuality or whatever, why do you not go all the way and wed me? It would probably be less expensive for you in the long run."

It surprised her that he did not laugh her to scorn. He pursed his lips and regarded her through slitted eyes. He raised the head of his cane to his lips and tapped at them gently.

In a musing tone, he said: "You believe I could captivate you?" It was not said as though he expected an answer.

She blushed. "You embarrass me! It was only a remark to illustrate a point."

"But it is not beyond the realm of possibility."

She did not answer and looked away.

"Very well, it is a bargain," he declared. "I accept."

Her head came up with a jerk, and she stared at him in open-mouthed consternation.

"My lord, your facetiousness is not appreciated in the least! I do not care to jest about anything so solemn."

"I am not jesting and, since you say you do not, I take you at your word. Please to set the date."

A frown of incredulity distorted her countenance and she stared hard at him.

His face was quite sober and he was gazing at her intently.

"My lord, what madness is this? You know nothing of me. My lineage, my station are far inferior to yours. As for mutual respect and affection, we have known each other for some twenty minutes. It is to laugh! If this is, in truth, a proposal of marriage, I categorically reject it and feel perfectly silly to have to do so!"

"Why?" he asked calmly.

"I do not know you and, of course, I do not love you."

"But you do know me—at least the very worst side of me as it has been conveyed to you by all the gossip. As for love, that is no prerequisite for marriage."

"It is for me!"

"Well then, I shall have to make you fall in love with me if that is what you wish."

The discussion was become far too ridiculous and Miss Brown was beside herself with uncertainty, for he was forcing her to the effort of fending off this outrageous importunity.

"My lord, I beg of you to cease this unseemly jest. I am sure there are thousands upon thousands of females who would welcome your advances. Unfortunately, I am not one of them, nor can I understand what about me constitutes such a prize in your eyes."

"You are different. I have never met anyone like you before. My wealth and my title make no impression upon you. If you should come to me, it will be because you love Tony Quarnell, not because you are desirous of becoming the Marquise of Montreat."

"But I do *not* love you!"

"I will gamble on it that you will eventually."

"No!"

There was silence for a moment.

A calculating look came into his eyes. Very slowly, he said: "I could force you to my will— here and now."

She felt a cold clutch of fear and attempted to

disguise her sudden alarm by saying staunchly: "Here? In a shop open to the public?"

With a vicious snort of laughter, he went to the door, shot the bolt and draped his handkerchief over the small window. Then he turned and, standing in the entranceway, said: "Here and now!"

"I-I b-beg you will not, my lord," she stammered, all atremble.

"That is all you will do—merely beg?"

"I know I cannot resist you. I can only entreat you," she pleaded.

He came towards her.

She put out her hand. "My lord, I-I will marry you if you insist—only, please, not this!"

He emitted a hard bark of laughter. "What need will there be for that, after?"

She let out a moan and sank to the floor. "Oh God!" she cried and swooned.

৯

A coarse burning taste in her mouth made her gasp and swallow, and the fire of it burned its way to her stomach. She came to with a choking gasp and pushed away the hand that was holding the brandy flask to her lips. Opening her eyes, she saw him kneeling beside her and she cringed away from him.

The marquis' face, grim in its expression, was inches away from her own. Even as she regarded him with horror, his face broke into a smile of relief.

"Welcome back, Miss Brown, from the land of terror. For all your wit, you are the worst sort of goose. When I would be truthful with you, you call me dishonest and, when I am but jesting, you faint away with fright. How very odious I must appear to you, I am only just beginning to appreciate."

She realized they were on the floor, and she was seated in his lap with his arm about her shoulder. Immediately she began to struggle free, but the pressure of his arm increased and held her immobile.

"Now, please, you are still too weak to rise. Rest easily where you are. You could not be safer, and I do not mind in the least."

But she could not relax. She had heard much of the ways of the noble rakes and roués—and of them all the Marquis of Montreat was the most notorious. She was sure it was all over with her.

"Dammit, girl! Has my jest broken your spirit? I said for you to rest. You are as tight as a spring!"

"M-my l-lord, your touch—after your threat— is less than consoling."

"I suppose I did go too far with it," he remarked with a sigh. "Very well, see if you can rise."

She made the effort, but her knees felt like so

much water and she would have fallen had it not been for his strong arms quickly about her as he rose with her.

He held her to him in support, and she, weak woman that she was, could only cling to him, her head on his breast, weeping.

He said nothing but searched in a pocket for his handkerchief. He searched the other and then patted both but in vain until she raised her head and said, with a tearful gurgle: "You placed it across the window in the door."

She was not crying now and there was a twisted smile on her face, but her eyes were running and her cheeks were damp.

He smiled down at her shamefacedly. "Can you stand, now?"

She nodded.

He released her, watched to see that she did not falter, then went over to the door and fetched the handkerchief. He presented it to her and she quickly put it to use.

"My dear Miss Brown, I must owe you a great debt for this odious prank. It is no excuse, but I did it because I wished to see you humbled. That I succeeded will give me many a sleepless night, for it is not a memory I shall ever have pride or pleasure in."

He took out his wallet and handed it to her.

"This is not the full payment. It is merely an earnest of my intention to meet whatever demand you will deem it necessary to make upon me for this grievous insult I have offered you."

She eyed the wallet. It was thick and it was tempting. She did not doubt that she could live in comfort for three full years on its contents. So that her hands might not betray her longing, she put them behind her back as she shook her head.

"You were very convincing in the role, my lord —or perhaps because of all I have heard of you, I wished to believe you were so foul. In either case, I acted the part of a silly girl. I accept your explanation and apology and will not trouble you further."

"How are you called, Miss Brown?"

"I am Elizabeth to my friends, my lord."

"Ah! How very appropriate! It is a name that suits you well, my dear. I would add that few who wear it these days can do it justice. Indeed, you are, truly, Elizabeth!" he declared, making a deep bow in emphasis of his admiration.

"You overdo the genuflection, my lord. I am not of the blood royal," she declared.

He straightened up with a great laugh. "Now that is my girl!" he exclaimed. "I am forgiven?"

"Yes, my lord. Good day, my lord."

"Oh no, you do not get rid of me so quickly!"

"Quickly? It feels like an age! Surely you have important business in other quarters, my lord."

"But that is why I have come. I have business with you! I shall not believe it if you deny you are not skilled at appraising manuscripts and books for their value, and I'll not be at all surprised if you are a great expert at cataloguing them into the bargain."

"And if I should be?"

"Then I have come to the right place. I recently acquired, by inheritance from an old curmudgeon of an uncle, a dreary place in the neighborhood of Bath. He was a great hand for accumulating all sorts of odds and ends of parchments and great volumes. I would enlist your services to put the rat's nest in order and inform me of any great curiosity or thing of value you might discover amongst them."

She cocked her head at him. "After this episode, do you think I would come alone to an estate of yours?"

"Why not? You did forgive me."

"True, but that is not to say I have lost my mind! My lord, I do not trust you."

He smiled and nodded his head. "Aye, and you are right not to. Since I had the overwhelming pleasure of holding you in my arms I am sorely tempted to repeat the experience."

Elizabeth put up a hand in alarm and backed off a step.

"My lord!"

"I am tempted, but that is all. Do not worry. I

am on my best behavior with you for as long as you like."

"That will be forever!"

He sighed. "That is an awfully long time. Will you accept the commission?"

"It is out of the question! I most certainly will not stir in that direction without a proper chaperon—"

"But I have given you my word," he stated, with a frown. "Do you think I am less than honorable?"

She smiled. "Oddly enough, no! I think you lack a sense of proportion in your sense of humor is all."

He appeared relieved. "Then why—?"

"Because, my lord, my reputation would be worth less than nothing were I to sojourn with you without someone to guard it."

"But I'll not be staying there with you."

"Will you be in Bath?"

"Of course."

"That is close enough. I'll not consider it without I have a chaperone."

"Very well. Take a chaperone."

"That was all supposition. Although I should like very much to accept the commission—I have a passion for old writings and such—it is still out of the question."

"Well, I should like to know why not!" he demanded. "I have made you a perfectly good business proposition. There are no strings attached if that is what is worrying you—ah! The money! What is your fee?"

"I could not say until I had some idea of the length of time I should be at the work."

"Say two months—six months! Say a year!"

"Oh, don't be silly! I could never be away for anything like that. I should lose my shop!"

He considered for a moment. "I'll buy you another."

"My lord!" she cried in indignation. "I thought you said this was a *business* proposition!"

"Very well. If you insist on strictly business, will £50 in your landlord's hand hold the place for you?"

She looked at him aghast. "Why that would be enough for almost two years rent!"

"Good."

"And my custom? Even if I were away for a month or so, I should have to start all over again. People have such short memories."

"Hire a clerk! Another £70 should do it."

"That is as much as I can earn in a good year! I have no such sum!"

"I have! My man of business will see to everything!"

"Well, it is impossible, so I pray you will not try to tempt me further."

"It is not impossible!" he declared. "I have met each and every one of your objections."

"My lord, I-I cannot afford to go on such a journey. I-I have not the funds to pay the fare, to say nothing at all of clothing and the expense of a companion."

He regarded her silently for a moment. Then he said, with a kindly smile: "And you are very proud, too, are you not? How I must have torn at your dignity before and, yet, there you stand, engaged in conversation with me as though I were quite a most respectable gentleman. Elizabeth—I am come to adore you!"

"I will settle for your respect and forgo the adoration."

"Of course. But you *will* take the commission!"

"No, I-I cannot!"

"I will not force you. I will never force you. But tell me you do not wish for this work and I shall leave."

"Of course I wish to do the work. What bibliophile would not?"

He smiled. "Then do it you shall!" He took out his wallet and put it into her hands, holding them together so that she could not let it go. "There is some £300 in it. Consider it an advance against your fee. It should cover your necessaries and more, I hope. If not, you may charge to my account. I shall arrange it. Do not worry about fares. You will go out to Bath in my light coach, with coachman and footman in attendance. If you wish, I'll see you supplied with maids, one for you and one for your companion. There is some sort of housekeeping staff at Gryfynskepe, and all of you should be quite comfortable there."

She was spellbound and could not speak. She could only shake her head in refusal.

"What? You still persist in your misguided obstinacy? What am I to do with you!"

"My Lord Marquis, it is too much! I do not know what you are at. Is this your way of buying me, still?"

"My dear, if I thought ten times these sums would buy you, I should make the expenditure without a qualm. No, Elizabeth, this is a straightforward offer and for important work to be accomplished. I'll not spare the expense to see it done."

Elizabeth completely discounted his introductory declaration and gave her attention to the proposed transaction. "But you can have such an appraisal at a fraction of the cost and done by the most eminent bookmen in London. Or for much less by their colleagues in Bath. I am no recognized authority in these matters. I should charge you £15, or perhaps £25 if it took more than a month to do, and consider myself handsomely paid."

"Thank you for the advice, but, tell me, are they more competent than you?"

"They must be! They are so affluent."

"What has that to say to anything? I am even

more affluent, but that does not make me an expert in anything at all, necessarily!"

"Well, I daresay, given the opportunity, they would not find me lacking. I have been engaged in this business since I was a child."

"I am pleased to know it, for it makes you the best qualified."

"How so, my lord?"

"I need someone I know I can trust."

"How can you say that? You do not know the first thing about me!"

"Do you think I have been talking to you for over an hour and have learned nothing?"

"You can have learned nothing I did not tell you, my lord."

"Then, immediately, I shall learn something more. Elizabeth, can I trust you?"

She stared at him in great consternation. Then she hung her head and said nothing.

"You have not answered me," he said.

She laughed weakly but still did not look at him. "To a question like that, what matters it how I answer?"

"It matters. Can I trust you, Elizabeth?"

"Yes, my lord," she murmured.

"Miss Brown, will you do me the honor of dining with me this evening?"

She looked up at him, and there was a warm smile

upon her face. "How will you explain a shop-keeper to your friends, Lord Montreat?"

"At Claridge's, I need not explain anything. In your case, they must know at once."

"That I am your latest mistress, I do not doubt."

He smiled. "Not at Claridge's, my dear."

"Do you tell me gentlemen have not been known to bring their mistresses to Claridge's? I am not so green. Even Almack's is not beyond that practice."

His eyes turned a little hard. "You will learn, Elizabeth, that the Marquis of Montreat does not bring his mistresses to Claridge's nor does he escort them to Almack's."

She regarded him with an air of puzzlement. "Am I to understand you intend me a compliment?"

"No, for you would not believe me if I did."

"Well, thank you, in any case, my lord, and for the invitation, too, but of course I may not accept."

He let out a breath as though his temper was being frayed. "I am beginning to expect that everything I suggest must become a subject for debate. Is it that you fear me still?"

"It is that I have not a thing to wear to any place so grand as Claridge's."

"You have money, now. Buy what you need and stop making complaint. You are beginning to sound like a wife!"

She looked horrified. "But I cannot spend it for such a purpose! I have not earned it!"

"God, give me patience! You are now in my employ. Would you shame me by appearing to less advantage than my servants?"

"You wish me to appear in livery?" she asked, trying to maintain a sober mien, but her eyes were dancing and they quite gave her away.

His lordship stood up very straight and looked down his nose at her with half-lidded eyes. "Pre—cisely," he drawled. "I always clothe my commissioners in fine silks and high fashion—bah! Look you and see to it you appear in nothing less! Come, I will introduce you to Madame Charmelle's establishment. I do not know a finer."

"Nor more expensive!"

He threw up his hands. "Miss Brown, if you will go on in this fashion, I am forced to conclude you do not wish the commission after all."

She hastened to assure him. "Oh, my lord, I do! And it warms my heart that you should wish to treat me to so fine a diversion as dinner at Claridge's, but it is not in the least necessary. The commission and the extravagant expenditure you are preparing to incur are all I could wish!"

He smiled sourly. "Very well. I see that it is because I am so low in your esteem, you deem a friendship between us as unthinkable."

"You mistake my meaning, sir!" she exclaimed in indignation. "Despite your gallantry, I am sure you can have no wish for my company when I can only prove an embarrassment to you."

Suddenly her mood lightened and she smiled. In a completely different tone, she said: "You know, my lord, to be accounted only a *friend* to the notorious Marquis of Montreat must be a rare accomplishment, indeed, if one is a female. Don't you think so?"

He laughed with delight at the setdown. "Elizabeth, I give you my solemn word, I *shall* be honored by your company."

"My lord, you make it devilishly difficult to refuse you."

"I will admit *I* have never had such difficulty before. I am at my wits' end to make it *impossible* for you to refuse me!"

Elizabeth let out a gurgle of laughter. "Very well, my lord, but only on condition that I pay for my purchases."

"Naturally. I'll see that the bills are presented to you in due course. What you have got in that"—he indicated the wallet—"might barely cover the cost of your gown for this evening, with shoes and hat and whatever."

"Oh dear!" she exclaimed in agitated surprise. "I shall be in debt to you forever!"

"Now that would be a pleasant prospect to contemplate," he said. "But I am sure you will see to it that your fees to me will never allow it."

"I could never—"

"I am fast losing patience with you, Miss Brown! My carriage awaits!"

"Yes, my lord!" exclaimed Elizabeth in mock terror. "And if I do not go quickly, I daresay it will turn into a pumpkin."

"More like, I shall turn into a frog!"

ॐ

"Beth, where have you been? And what have you there? And who is *he?* And—and what have you done to your *hair?!!*" cried Mary Vernon, as Beth trouped into the chambers they shared, followed by a tall and somewhat reserved male attendant carrying a great load of parcels and boxes.

The man laid the parcels in a heap upon a sofa that doubled as a bed and turned to Beth. "Will there be anything else, my lady?"

There was a queer, questioning look in her eyes as she glanced up at him. Then she drew up her reticule and extracted a pound note from it. She offered it to him saying: "Thank you, Cowles. That will be all."

He bowed. "Very good, my lady. And I thank you, but my lord does not permit his people to accept gratuities."

"Oh! Well, then, thank you again, Cowles. I hope I have not been a trouble to you."

"Indeed, it was my pleasure, my lady." His rigid features relaxed for a moment as he smiled. He bowed and withdrew.

When the door had closed behind him, Beth murmured: "How very strange!"

"Indeed, it is a deal more than strange! Your hair! What have you done with your hair? It is perfectly adorable on you—but all those little curls! It must have cost a fortune! You could never have done it yourself!"

Beth smiled with great glee as she went over to the small mirror above the tiny side table against the wall. Peering into it, she patted her coiffure here and there and then pirouetted to face Mary.

"Do you truly like it, cousin? You must have yours done, too."

"But, child, have you gone mad? Where's the money to come from?" she pleaded, almost in tears.

Beth chuckled aloud, dipped her hand into her reticule and scattered notes of various denominations all about, like some impish figure of plenty.

Mary was aghast.

"Oh, great heavens! You sold the shop!" she exclaimed.

"No," said Beth with a vigorous shake of her head as she bent to collect the litter of bank notes. "Better than that!"

"Then where did you get it? Tell me quickly before I am driven clear out of my mind!"

Beth went over to the divan and she removed the parcels, setting them down on the floor. She sat down and Mary came to sit beside her.

"Oh dear, I do not know where to begin!"

Mary exclaimed: "Try to be logical for once. Start with your hair. How much did it cost you?"

"Not a thing!"

"You *never* did it yourself!" protested Mary.

"It was the hairdresser at Madame Charnelle's, with Madame herself overseeing it."

Mary's mouth gaped open. "Why in the world should she do a thing like that for you?"

"Because, dear cousin, a customer who spends a £1,000 in her establishment must be entitled to *some* free courtesy in return."

"Oh dear," moaned Mary, "my poor head! I am afraid to ask you where you had the money from, but I pray you will tell me anyway."

"Oh, do not be a ninny, Mary! Where would I get a £1,000?"

"That is exactly my point!"

"I charged it all on account."

"You charged it all on account? That *is* what you said? *You* charged it all on account! Madame Charnelle does not know you from Eve, so you must have charged it to someone else—Oh my! That is positively gorgeous!" she broke off to exclaim as

Beth lifted out from one of the parcels a bright green gown, richly brocaded with gold threads all over.

Beth stood up, pressed it against her form and whirled about the room to wind up before the mirror once more.

"Isn't it lovely though?" she asked over her shoulder.

But Mary was now busily engaged in unpacking the other parcels. With each discovery of the different treasures they contained, she let out a gasp.

A pair of golden slippers was in one hand and a generously brimmed green hat, with a bright yellow plume of great size, was in her other as she turned in speechless amazement to confront her cousin.

Beth, catching sight of her awestruck countenance in the mirror, turned about with a little laugh.

"All right, Mary, I will tell you all about it. All this was charged to the account of the Marquis of Montreat, and I shall pay for it out of the moneys I am to receive for appraising a library for him."

Mary put one hand to her forehead, which was deeply furrowed as though with great pain, and put her other out to her cousin.

"Stop! Stop a moment! The Marquis of Montreat—my Lord *Rakehell?*"

"Yes."

Mary shook her head and closed her eyes. "He

is going to pay you £1,000 to appraise a library? One of you is mad—at least! Are the books printed with golden ink on ivory leaves?"

Beth laughed. "Oh, that is very good of you! No, it is not anything like that at all. The library is near Bath, and I am to receive a fee, plus he is to pay my expenses. He insists that all this is a part of my expenses."

"You have become his mistress! But no, that is hardly likely!"

Beth came to sit by her cousin. "Mary, prepare yourself. You have been like a mother to me, and what I have to say is going to come as the greatest shock. But hear me out and stay my friend. Do not desert me when I have need of you more than ever before."

Her face turned wistful. "Strange as it may seem —I still cannot credit it—my Lord Montreat is bound and determined that I become his mistress, and I am bound and determined to make the most of it."

"Oh no, my love! Do not say so! You do not have to sell yourself to that vile wretch! The shop helps us to keep body and soul together, and we have been content!"

"It is not the money, Mary. It is Montreat, himself. I can well understand how he has gained his reputation. Yes, I daresay he is a vile wretch, but it is of little moment, for I am sure I shall fall in love with him and be lost like so many others before me."

"You cannot be serious, child! You know what he is. His name is common gossip! It is not too late. Return all this!"

"You do not understand! Perhaps I am more fortunate than most. I have been able to withstand him and, with your help, I shall be able to withstand him longer. You must come with me to Bath! Please say that you will!"

"But what can I do if your mind is made up?"

"It will be enough if you are about." She sighed. "He is everything I could want in a husband, but I am not such a fool to aspire to *that* eminence. Something a deal less will have to do." She sighed again. "I daresay he is the most charming man I have ever met."

She laughed. "Considering his behavior towards me, that is a far greater compliment to him than you can imagine."

"Why, what did he do?"

"Oh, nothing. I do not care to say. But you see, he could not get at me directly, so he has concocted this Banbury tale about a library in Bath. It is only a ruse but, as he is willing to pay the piper for a merry dance, I shall do my best to make it a long, or an expensive one." She shrugged. "Had it been anyone else, I would have refused without qualification. But my Lord Montreat—I can put him off, but I know I cannot do so forever—and he is not one to lose sight of his prey."

She began again, in a rush: "So you see, since it will come to that in the end, the longer we can play out this string the better for us."

"Are you in love with the fellow or are you not?"

"I suppose I am already. I felt it there in the shop when I rested in his lap—"

"You what?!!"

"Oh, dear," said Beth with a little chuckle, "I made a slip. No, do not ask me about it, for I shall not say another word."

Mary frowned. "I do not understand more than a little of what you have told me and, of that little, I have less liking than understanding. For example, why should the Marquis of Montreat show any interest at all in Beth Brown, an inconsequential shopkeeper, when it has always been only great beauties that his name has ever been linked with?"

"I have no idea. It could be that he has lost his taste for the grand game and wishes to sample a more modest quarry."

"And believing this, you will allow yourself to be possessed by him?"

"Mary, it is no manner of use to debate it. I know what he has been and what he is. My feeling for him has not blinded me. But I suppose every woman hopes, when she discovers the right man, that no matter how he has treated others, he will be differ-

ent with her. Oh, will you listen to me! One would
think I was a mere schoolgirl, I babble on so! It will
be the same for me just as it has been for the others.
The love of my lord marquis is a very temporary
thing at best. Oh, why did I ever have to meet him!"
She laid her head upon her cousin's shoulder and
began to sob.

"There, there, child, you have every cause to
weep!" said Mary consolingly, with a catch in her
voice.

"I am not weeping for myself! I weep for him!
He must be the unhappiest of men to have to hunt
so for love and never to find it."

Beth eased herself back to a sitting position and
mopped at her eyes. "You will come to Bath with
me?"

"You know I will, but will he allow it?"

"I demanded it of him."

Mary bestowed a queer look on Elizabeth but
refrained from commenting. "What of the shop?"
she asked. "I am sure we must lose it, for I have a
strange feeling it will be a while before we see it
again."

"His man of business will see to it."

Mary threw up her hands. "Well, I never heard
the like!" she exclaimed. "For all the trouble he is
taking, why does he not marry you and have done
with it?"

Elizabeth laughed. "Yes, that is exactly what I asked of him."

"I pray you will not stop there! For heaven's sake, what did he answer?"

"He quite agreed, but I laughed in his face. We had not been speaking but a few minutes and he offered. I tell you the man is without conscience. He will say anything if it will gain him his end."

"My dear, this is the most confusing business it has ever been my misfortune to be associated with. Someday you will have to try to make it all clear to me. For the nonce, my poor head is so hopelessly addled, I could not take the sum of two and two. When do you think you will see him again?"

Beth leaped to her feet in panic. "Great heavens! Here we have been at prosing away the afternoon, and he is coming for me this evening! Dear, oh dear! I must rush or I shall never be ready! Be a dear and help me! He is taking me to dine at Claridge's, and I have not even begun to dress! I shall never do it by myself in time!"

Mary let out a groan. She was not a half-dozen years the elder, but suddenly she felt very old indeed.

Lord Montreat helped Elizabeth mount up into the carriage and got in beside her.

"I do not know whether I should feel cheated or not," he said, as the driver urged up the horses.

She turned to him. "What do you mean, my lord?"

"I cannot believe you are the same young lady I met this morning. You are different—lovely, in fact!"

Very matter-of-factly, Elizabeth pointed out: "It is this gown, these clothes. They are lovely, not I."

"No, I think not. And I venture to say that your very formidable cousin agrees with me. I saw the look of pleasure in her eyes."

"Cousin Mary is formidable? How can she be? She loves me!"

He smiled. "Am I to understand that because she loves you, she cannot be formidable?"

"Of course. How else could it be?" responded Elizabeth.

"I believe I could put some holes in the reasoning behind that if I had a mind to, but I should prefer to carry it into a different channel. May I suggest then that, by your logic, it must follow that if some person is not formidable to you, he or she must love you?"

"I see nothing wrong with that conclusion, my lord."

"Do you find me formidable, Elizabeth?" he asked softly.

"Need you ask, my lord? Have you forgotten so quickly that scene in the shop?"

"But it was only a jest."

"A most formidable jest."

His lordship chuckled. "I see you are determined that it shall haunt me the rest of my life."

"Not at all, my lord. I have quite forgotten it, I assure you."

"I am so pleased to hear you say so," he remarked dryly.

Elizabeth clapped her gloved hands to her mouth in embarrassment. She peered at him over her hands and giggled. "I haven't, have I?"

He laughed and reached out to give her arm a squeeze.

She said: "Let us talk of something else so I *can* forget it."

"Elizabeth, I would ask a favor of you."

She looked at him, her face suddenly saddened. "So soon?" she asked plaintively.

He returned her a look of bewilderment. "What do you mean 'so soon'?"

"Oh, nothing. What would you ask of me, my lord?"

"I should prefer you did not use my title."

"Oh." And there was great relief in her voice.

"But that is ridiculous! I cannot call you 'Montreat'!"

"Hardly! I am called 'Tony.'"

"Lord Tony?" She wrinkled her nose. "No, that is for a rake—Oh dear!" and she began to giggle.

His lordship laughed heartily. "Did you say that on purpose, you little devil?" he demanded, still chuckling.

"No, my lord, it was the inspiration of the moment. Let me see. My Lord Anthony. Is not that better than my Lord Tony?"

"Plain 'Tony' will do fine."

"But that would be sheer impudence! What must people think?"

"Exactly what I wish them to think. And as for impudence, you are very long in that suit. You have been at that game from the first moment you laid eyes on me."

"What do you wish people to think?" she asked.

"You will see," he said.

శ్రీ

Elizabeth had become strangely quiet for the remainder of their drive and she was not happy as his lordship guided her into the Claridge dining hall. She thought there could be no point in not comply-

ing with his wish. Her relationship to him would
come out in the end. If he wished it revealed sooner
rather than later, so be it. Nevertheless, the sparkle
of the evening had become quite tarnished for her.

The maître d'hotel came to them and offered a
choice of seating from amongst the tables laid out
on the floor.

"Or perhaps the marquis prefers a private room,"
he suggested, not very sure of himself as he tried
to size up Lord Montreat's lady friend. A new face
was always a problem to him for, more often than
not, the lady had no wish to be noticed particularly.
This one, he thought, seemed to be one of "those."

The marquis turned to his lady and said, a little
loudly: "Which shall it be, Elizabeth?"

"Whatever you wish, Tony," she said, a little
above a whisper.

"What's that, my dear?" exclaimed the marquis,
bringing his hand to his ear. "I fear the night air
has affected my hearing."

Elizabeth fought back her tears as she said quite
distinctly: "Wherever you wish, Tony!"

"Thank you, my dear. Armand, that table over
there will do."

Armand bowed and, with great relief in his voice,
requested: "My lady, please to follow me."

Elizabeth looked to Tony, her eyes wide in surprise.

He grinned back at her and slowly winked his

eye. He took her by the elbow and led her over to a table at which two couples were seated.

The gentlemen immediately arose. They were of an age with Tony. Elizabeth thought the smiles of greeting they wore appeared tinged with an air of incredibility.

One of them hailed: "Tony, old chap, delighted to see you! It has been ages. I'll not ask where you have been keeping yourself. It is quite evident."

Tony then introduced Elizabeth to his friends. Naturally, they were all on fire to know something of Miss Elizabeth Brown, but Tony put them off. He graciously refused their invitation to join them, and he and Elizabeth withdrew to their own table.

Armand assisted Elizabeth to seat herself, took their order and went off.

Elizabeth did not dare to look at Tony but kept her eyes on her plate.

"You do not trust me at all, do you?" asked Tony.

Elizabeth made no reply.

"My dear, I am not angry with you. I think I am irked at myself. My detestable sense of humor, you know. But I did tell you that I never brought my mistresses here, do you recall?"

"Yes, my lord."

"Tony."

"Yes, Tony."

"You can at least look at me. What will my friends think?"

She looked up and her expression was troubled. "What do they think? They seemed so surprised—as though they could not believe their eyes."

He chuckled. "Aye, they were surprised all right. I daresay by tomorrow all London will be surprised. Who is Elizabeth Brown? will be the watchword of the ton for weeks."

"Why are you doing this to me, Tony?"

"Don't you think it is quite a jest?"

"I told you before, I have no taste for your jests."

Tony looked at her and smiled. "I suppose I had that coming, but this one will not harm you in any way. I swear it!"

She smiled back uncertainly. "I suppose if I am to spend any time with you, I must be able to take your idiosyncracies in stride."

"That is one thing I lo-like about you, Elizabeth. No matter how I may try you, in the end, you have a smile for me."

"The antics of small boys and imbeciles are oft-times amusing. Until I know you better, I hesitate to say which of these you are."

"A small boy I surely am not. That leaves you no choice at all."

She chuckled. Then feigning a sigh of mild distress, she declared: "Ah yes, you must be right, and I have caught the contagion from you, or why else am I sitting here with you? I think I know what you are at."

"Splendid! You must tell me, for I am not quite sure myself."

"Oh, you are an imbecile!"

That was the last bit of intelligent conversation they held at table for, between the serving of the viands and people visiting their table to pay their respects to the marquis while they eyed his companion with undisguised curiosity, it became impossible to put two sensible words together.

When they had finished, Tony said: "I do not think we can improve the situation any further by remaining here. I hope you have enjoyed your dinner."

"Thank you, Tony. I could not help but. I have always dreamed of coming here, but on a shopkeepers' income it was remote beyond possibility that I should."

"It was my pleasure; but now, my fair antiquarian, we have matters of business to discuss, and I should prefer not to do it here. There are certain details about Gryfynskepe I would have you know. It will help you in your searches."

"And what may they be?"

"Not here. There is cause to make me believe it wise if we discuss it in greater privacy. For this purpose, I suggest we return to my place on Park Lane."

"And spend the night, no doubt."

"Why, that is an excellent suggestion!" he exclaimed. "You have read my mind!"

"Certainly not the most difficult feat in the world," she retorted dryly. "But it was not a suggestion! If we must talk, it will have to be at my chambers in Bloomsbury. And do not think I am behind you in offering hospitality. You may spend the night there if you wish."

He chuckled. "Thank you, Elizabeth, but of course I would not dream of it. I suggested my place only out of consideration for the repose of your cousin."

"I understand you perfectly well. I suggest my place out of consideration for my repose, *you* will understand."

He eyed her critically, some of the humor draining from his face. "You certainly do not have much respect for your employer's wishes."

"It is not me you have purchased, Tony, only my services—Oh dear!" She laughed as her face turned a delicate pink. "I have done it again! But you know what I mean."

He arose abruptly and came round to her chair. "Come! We must leave!" he said roughly and he half-lifted her out of her seat. Grabbing her arm, he firmly propelled her out of the room. Without a pause, he snatched up their wraps and carried them along to the street where he helped her on with hers.

"I do declare, Tony, that was awfully rough of

you! I do not see that we shall be able to continue if that is how you receive my refusal! You marched me out of Claridge's as though I were some three-year-old little miss!"

"That had nothing to do with it! I had to! There you were all rosy-faced with embarrassment. People were bound to think that I had made you an indecent proposal!"

"Well, you had!"

"And you took it with all the aplomb of one who was well up before the world. Then you had to spoil it for no good reason at all except that your miserable tongue made its usual witless stumble. Oh, get into the carriage! I shall be glad to see you off to Bath. I have an idea I shall not know peace again until I do."

Elizabeth was puzzled to know whether he was truly annoyed or just funning as usual. She thought it wiser not to respond and entered the carriage as she was bid.

The marquis instructed his coachman to proceed to Bloomsbury.

Cousin Mary opened to them and, being in a

wrapper and night clothes, was all caught up in embarrassment as the marquis followed Elizabeth in.

She dipped into the mere suggestion of a curtsy to the marquis and immediately challenged her cousin: "Beth, why did you bring *him* here?"

"Would you have preferred I accepted his invitation to spend the night at *his* residence?"

"Oh. Oh!"

His lordship obviously enjoyed the exchange, for he laughed and Mary was covered with further confusion.

In an accusing tone, Tony exclaimed to Elizabeth: "So it is Beth! I am hurt that you never told me."

Beth ignored his remark. "Mary, his lordship has a wish to inform us of some circumstances concerning our impending visit to Bath. It is just as well you listen, too—if you do not object, Tony."

"Rather pointless, what?" he remarked, his gaze roving about the tiny set of chambers.

"I'll stop my ears if you prefer, your lordship, but I'll not leave this room!" snapped Mary.

"Mistress Mary, I should never prefer it. You do not know how it pleases me that you are to accompany Beth. I have not the least worry but that you will keep her safe."

"From all!" declared Mary with a pointed look.

The marquis bowed. "From all," he declared solemnly.

Beth was watching his face closely all this time. "My lord, you would put a Garrick to shame for the ease with which you dissemble your disappointment."

He chuckled. "Ah, but you are mistaken, my lady, for I have not been disappointed in you, yet."

"My lord, I am not your lady or anyone else's. To use such a title embarrasses me."

"I will cease my ladying you if you will desist from my lording me."

"As you wish, Tony."

"That is better."

"Whatever is going on?" exclaimed Mary. "I never heard of such a thing—Tony? Beth? My lord, such familiarity is most unseemly and undignified, I do protest!"

"My dear Cousin Mary, it is my dignity and I daresay I can do with it as I please!"

To be addressed as cousin by so grand a gentleman, for all his reputation, quite turned Mary's wits into confusion and rendered her wordless.

"Now then, if I may be seated, we shall get to this business at Gryfynskepe and then I shall leave you ladies to your rest.

"Gryfynskepe came into my possession two months ago at the demise of an old and crotchety uncle. It is comprised of an ancient house situated on a fair rise of ground overlooking Combe Hay, a village something over three miles to the southwest of Bath. I have visited it not very long ago and found it in a reasonable state of repair. There are two servants in residence, relict of my late uncle. They are man and wife, Baker by name. Considering Uncle Ethelbert's style of living, I do not imagine that the Bakers are paragons of virtue or service; therefore, you will be accompanied by a selection of my staff who will see to your comfort during your stay."

"All this for a female dealer in books is exceptional beyond anything, Tony, especially when you have known her but a day. I must say you do not count the cost in the pursuit of your pleasures."

Tony thought over her remark for a moment. Then he smiled and said: "My dear, I do not count the cost in the pursuit of anything I value, and there is something valuable at Gryfynskepe. I do not know what it is, but I have some idea of its worth."

"Do you say that all this is *not* a lure to put me at a disadvantage?" demanded Beth.

"If I were to agree that it is, would you still go?"

"Then why do you allow me to bring Mary with me?"

"Simply because you would not go if I forbade you to. Is it not so?"

"*I'd* not let her go!" broke in Mary fiercely, thereby saving Beth from having to respond.

Beth brought the conversation back: "Then you admit that you will try to take advantage of me."

He chuckled. "I should be lying if I denied it, but you have your protection. Now, if you would be kind enough to connive with me to defeat her vigilance, that would be a most interesting prospect." He leered outrageously as he said it and even Mary had to laugh.

He was still smiling as he continued: "You know perfectly well my intentions towards you, Beth. I have never troubled to hide them nor shall I ever. But that is not the purpose behind the visit to Gryfynskepe. It is still the same reason I came to your shop to consult with your late father.

"Gryfynskepe is not such a property as fills me with any pride of ownership, and so, after looking it over, I had it listed for sale. I should have been happy to have received two or three thousand pounds for it. The land is too steep for husbandry, and the house itself is long past its best years; only its proximity to Bath justifies even that sum.

"To my great surprise, a realtor made an offer of £14,000 for it. Now, if he had offered four or five thousand I should have leaped to accept, but fourteen thousand was so ridiculously high that it gave me to think. I came to the conclusion that something in or about Gryfynskepe must be worth at least £20,000 to somebody, and I vowed to get to the bottom of it.

"I repaired at once to the place and examined and measured it from the cellars to the rooftop. I discovered nothing out of the ordinary. Oh, there was a priest hole, of course, and a secret entrance from the outside leading up to it. I cannot abide such nonsense, so I had it all ripped out and redone. I am satisfied that there is nothing hidden away to explain the strange offer.

"Now Uncle Ethelbert, if one were inclined to be charitable, might be deemed to have been an anti-quarian of parchments but, in actual fact, was neither more nor less than a collector of trash. When you see the state in which he kept his collection, you will appreciate it that he was not driven by any fondness for the particular bits and pieces he suc-ceeded in heaping together in his lifetime. But that is not to say that, unbeknownst to himself, he did not manage to pick up an item or two of special value, now hidden away in the vast dust heaps of his collection.

"There are two rooms stacked to the ceilings with parchment and I warn you to be careful, for I am sure they will come tumbling down upon you like some great avalanche if you are not. The work will be trying, and I daresay you should equip your-self with strong glasses and bright lamps. I am sure that you will need them, and they are not to be found at Gryfynskepe."

"Then it is a genuine commission?"

He looked at Beth intently. "You doubted it?"

"You confuse me."

He shook his head. "Now I am confused. You must have believed I intended to trap you, yet you accepted the commission. Your question is proof to me that you have not believed a word that I have said. If you did not trust me and do not still, it escapes me what your purpose in continuing is."

"I am fascinated by parchment."

"Now that is a whopper! I have only just informed you that parchment was involved."

"We are keeping Cousin Mary from her rest."

"I see." He rose to his feet. "Cousin Mary, my apologies. I shall take my leave."

Beth accompanied him to the door.

"Tony, you did say you would reside in Bath during our stay?"

"I did."

"Will—will we see anything of you?"

"On the weekends I shall come for you and Cousin Mary, and you will be my guests until Monday. I wish you to see Bath, and there are a number of people I shall want you to meet. There will be plenty of time for it."

"I do not see how. Two rooms full of manuscripts must call for all my efforts."

"There is no great rush. You will work as it pleases you but not on the weekends. They are mine."

Beth shrugged. "You realize the longer it takes the more I shall charge you."

"Since you are very heavily in debt to me already, you had better take all the time you can."

"What is the sum of my indebtedness to you?"

"When all the bills are rendered, I will let you know."

"My lord, I do not think the game is worth it for you."

"Perhaps not. But just to determine that point, it may be, my lady."

"Good night, Tony."

"Good night, my love—and pleasant dreams, Cousin Mary!" he called lightly over her shoulder.

*

"Come," said Mary, "let me help you off with your gown."

As the glamorous creation came up over her head and she emerged from it, her hair all tousled, Beth appeared to be lost in thought.

"I cannot make him out, though my life depended on it," she mused.

Mary sniffed. "I will admit that for charm of manner and appearance, he has no superior, but it is a positive shame that such a ravening wolf should be allowed to parade himself as such a paragon of gentility in all the comeliness of an Apollo. Thank heaven we know him for what he is and I, for one, counsel you to flee from this snare he is laying out for you."

"But is it truly so? You heard him. He cannot be prevaricating. Two rooms stuffed with documents, he said. It must be so. It is too gross a tale not to be. And I hardly think that he would go to the trouble of collecting such a great store of parchment just as a lure for me. That is not sensible and he is a sensible man—and considerate beyond any fault."

"More trappings! My dear girl, you judge him too lightly indeed. There is a purpose to his charm and kindliness, and you must not lose sight of it. Oh, he is an enchanter, right enough!" She turned a little pink as she continued. "For all that I know of him, I am ashamed to admit that I was not unaffected by him. Cousin Mary! Imagine anyone taking the trouble to ingratiate an old crone like me!"

"Oh, Mary!" cried Beth, as she dropped the great flimsy hat into its box and turned to take her cousin into her embrace. "How dare you speak so ill of yourself! Old crone, indeed! If you did devote yourself to me less selflessly, you could be quite a handsome woman, yourself. If only you would make the effort!"

"Fiddlesticks! It is enough for me to worry about you. Who would there be to keep me from falling into the traps men set for us? Surely not you! Look at you! You fancy yourself smitten with this handsome devil. Heaven only knows what would become of you if I were not here to foil him!"

"You will admit he is interested in me for something beyond this business of parchments?"

"Well, you will admit he is not the first to importune you with an indecent proposal. You are no great beauty, Beth, but I have been aware for the longest time that you have a quality—it is an elusive thing—that men, even such a high-flyer as my Lord Montreat, find immensely appealing. But you also have a good head on your shoulders and I never feared that it would be turned to your disgrace until now. This monster with his glib charm and address—oh, how glib that man is!—if I did not know him for my Lord Rakehell, I could swear he had a proper *tendre* for you. It is a *tendre* he bears for you, but there is no honor he intends by it. 'Good night, my love' rolls from his lips so easily that one would think the banns were to be posted on the morrow. You know better than that, I am sure."

Beth sadly smiled. "Yes, I know better than that, dear Mary. But I also know that I shall do all in my power to stay close to him, come what may. After tonight, I am in no doubt whatsoever. I love Tony."

"What was so special about tonight, may I ask? Good heavens, girl, think what you are about! The first day of your acquaintanceship is not over yet! You cannot be enamored of him so soon!"

"Before we went into Claridge's, he insisted I address him as 'Tony.' Indeed, my heart sank, for how must I appear before the world, I, Beth Brown, of threadbare gentility to pretend to such impertinent familiarity with the great Montreat? I was sure he was forcing me into the role of mistress before his friends even if it were not so in fact."

"Oh, how painful it must have been for you!"

"Yes, I was on the verge of tears at his perfidy, but when the embarrassment came it was for a completely different reason. I could see that the maître d'hotel was hard put to make anything of me until Tony practically forced me to address him by his first name. It needs must be just 'Tony,' not my Lord Anthony or even Lord Tony. Immediately, the maître was all easy grace and addressed me as 'my lady'! And his friends! They kept visiting our table all evening and appeared to be quite taken with Miss Elizabeth Brown, and there was not the slightest hint of ribaldry in the manner. If my Lord Montreat was my betrothed, I could not have been treated with greater respect."

"But, Beth, how did he ever explain you to them?"

"He did not. Oh, he is so very clever! He parried and turned aside every inquiry regarding me and in such a way as incurred no offense—and that is something I still do not understand. He himself is beyond being abashed by anyone or anything, you will admit. He cannot care a crumb for the world's opinion, and so I am forced to conclude that his adroitness was exercised solely to preserve me from embarrassment. After all, there was little else they could think if once they learned I was an insignificant seller of books, and one could hardly blame them—but a moment! *Was* it just for my benefit? Montreat's taste is legendary. Perhaps he is not so immune to opinion. Would it not be quite a comedown for Montreat if his friends came to understand that my Lord Rakehell's latest conquest was poor little me, a penniless Bloomsbury shopkeeper?

"Oh, Mary, now I do not know what to believe! Did he preserve my identity from his friends for my sake or his own?"

"I hardly think that *that* is to the point, Beth! What I admire in him is the lengths the man will go to accomplish his ends."

"Yes, one is forced to admire his great ability."

"Or his experience!" amended Mary.

"Well, I believe it is more than base passion that has aroused his interest." In a voice thrilling with emotion, Beth went on to declare: "Sometime in the future he will make known to me his love for me, and I shall be the happiest female in Christendom!"

"And for how long do you think that the idyll will last?" asked Mary disdainfully.

"For a moment, for an hour—for a week, if I am lucky. What does it matter? Do I have any greater prospect for happiness?"

"Oh, if only we were not so poor!" lamented Mary.

"But we are!" And Beth laughed bitterly. "And even if we were not, this is not the sort of happiness that can be bought. Rich or poor, it would make no difference!"

"But think what it will be like afterwards! You will be but one of the many females he has possessed and cast aside."

"Oh, I am sure I shall hate him for doing the same with me, but at least we will be better off than we are now. My Lord Montreat, for all his faults, is not known to be tight in his pockets."

"Beth, you are in alt tonight! I do not think you know what you are saying. Go to bed! Tomorrow is a new day and rest may give you the wisdom to forgo this expedition to Bath."

Beth kissed her cousin. "Yes, I am weary and would sleep. But never doubt it! Until my Lord Tony casts me off of his own volition, *I* shall never let go of him!"

The next morning, both Beth and Mary went over to open the shop. They thought it wise to get things in order if they were to leave for Bath.

When they arrived, two gentlemen descended from a waiting Sefton landau. The tall black figure of the marquis was unmistakable. His companion was a young man of sober mien.

His lordship gave them a cheerful greeting and introduced them to Mr. Algernon Farrell, the marquis' man of business, who was to act in their interest while they were away.

They all entered the shop together and began at once to discuss the arrangements that were to be made.

This took some time, most of which was taken up with familiarizing Mr. Farrell with what the shop contained and where it was located. At an unobserved signal from his lordship, Mr. Farrell summarized for Elizabeth the major steps he would take to insure that the shop did not suffer in her absence and wound up the little conference by promising faithfully to consult her if any questions arose.

Elizabeth had to be satisfied with that because the marquis, all impatience, whisked them away to the grandest shops in London so that the ladies could provide themselves with all manner of garments he deemed necessary for their proper appearance in Bath.

Beth pleaded with my lord to seek out more modest establishments, but he would not listen. He seemed to gain considerable enjoyment at the effect the outrageous prices had upon his protegées. Very specifically, Beth objected to his purchasing three lovely ball gowns in her name. He informed her quite coolly that as he expected to escort her to the Pump Room and the Upper Rooms, he'd be eternally damned if she did not appear appropriately dressed for the occasion. Since his idea of "appropriate" verged upon what even a wealthy countess might have considered exorbitant, she got nowhere with him at all. It was no manner of use to point out to him that she was of the dregs of the gentry in station, and everyone must question the source of the funds for the clothes on her back. He countered that as she was so expert as to command the patronage of the Marquis of Montreat, it was not to be wondered at that she was paid handsomely for the expert services and advice that she rendered.

"Precisely, my lord—Tony. It is their opinion of what my expert services consist of that bothers me!"

He laughed. "Even after Claridge's, do you still think I am careless of your reputation?"

She blushed.

"Then be at ease. They will believe neither more nor less than what I wish them to believe."

And he appeared to be as good as his word, even as they passed from shop to shop spending like some young salt, flush with a voyage's earnings and but newly ashore. He carefully instructed the various proprietors that Miss Brown would honor their invoices when rendered. His simple statement was a magic invocation, for without a murmur, Miss Brown was served and fitted as though she were the greatest lady.

৪๑

In the usual course of events past, the ton had learned to take the adventures of Lord Montreat with members of the fair sex in stride. In their eyes he had proved himself a debaucher of the first water, and the recurring scandals in which he involved himself were of such a repetitious nature that his exploits had about as much of interest to them as the weather. It was enough, when two gossips met, be they male or female, if the one asked: "Have you heard the latest regarding Montreat?"

"With Lady Dennering?"

"Yes."

"Yes."

And they would then proceed to topics that promised some greater surprise or shock.

But the marquis' current involvement was certainly a horse of another color entirely, and no

longer could they be so smug about the outcome.
What Miss Brown's fate was to be they had little
doubt, but the marquis' way in the matter was suddenly become an object for the most intense
scrutiny.

In the past wagering, as it was concerned with
the marquis' way with his lights-o'-love, when there
was any, had to do with how long it would take
for his lordship to tire of his latest and take up with
another. It was never concerned with whether or
not he would be laid by the heels and be brought
to the altar. However, in this latest adventure there
was promise of a sort for a more interesting basis
for wagering.

That he had suddenly, and for the first time, appeared with Miss Brown at Claridge's was most unusual and not at all in accordance with his usual way.
Everyone knew that his infrequent visits to that
famous hotel never betokened a connection of any
intimate sort with his company. His companions,
without exception, were figures of high station and
advanced years, dear friends of his charming mother.
Occasionally they had been women of high fashion,
even of great beauty, but well known to all as his
particular friends and social equals—not that status
as such ever acted as a bar to his interest. But the
ladies that did appear with him at Claridge's were
hardly ever seen with him at any other time or place.

Miss Brown might have been accounted such a

person if she was beautiful or rich or famous, but she was not, by all reports, a beauty and no one had ever heard of her. That was enough to start the speculation off in full flower. It was known that she was on a first-name basis with the marquis and that was something to think about. Montreat was known to be a stickler for the proprieties. There were few females below the rank of peeress who dared to take such a liberty, and some of his more loquacious friends were quick to point out that no cyprian or actress would even think to accord him less than his station demanded. Miss Brown was, obviously, not of the nobility, but that she had appeared with him at Claridge's, she could not be accounted less than a gentlewoman—but for her to have called him "Tony"?

In a few days, as the news of Montreat's excursions to the shops where he had vouched for Miss Brown got about, the answer was clear to all. Moss would never flourish in Lord Tony's shadow. Obviously Miss Brown was an heiress of great wealth; there was no other possibility. And, since the marquis was no pauper in his own right, taking it all in all, Miss Brown must have been fabulously wealthy to have interested him. She had not a thing else to speak for her that anyone could discover.

And that was passing strange. For if she was so wealthy, then how could it be that no one had any idea of her background, her breeding and from whence she came? The more inquisitive went to work to remedy the lack and were even more surprised when it turned out that nobody who was anybody had the faintest idea of where she was staying in London! It was then that my Lord Montreat and his affairs became the subject of wagering to gladden the heart of the most hardened gamester. Everything from matrimony to the most scandalous speculations were deemed worthy of having great sums laid upon the altars of chance throughout the clubs on Piccadilly and St. James.

For three days these various sums lay stagnant. Not a bit of news, not a tidbit of gossip surfaced to settle the hundreds and hundreds of wagers. Finally it came to the lot of one dashing young blade, whose interest in life was comely shopkeeper's daughters and who of late, and for very good reason, had become a bibliophile—truly, it was not the books he loved, but the book vendor—it came to his lot to make a discovery that shed the much-needed light upon the identity and prospects of Miss Brown. Upon discovering that Miss Elizabeth Brown was no longer to be found at her shop in Bloomsbury and was not expected to be there for some time, he bethought himself of the coincidence of names and set himself to the task of confirming his wild suspicion. A stroll through the shops put him wise to the entire scheme and that evening, at his clubs, was stood round after round of liquid refreshment as he held forth upon his revelation and upon the cleverness he had exhibited in having tracked the information down.

Now, the gossips and the gamesters turned bitter. It was due as much to their universal disappointment that nothing odd at all was occurring—Lord Rakehell was up to his old tricks—as it was due to their sense of fair play being violated that Montreat had fallen so low as to prey upon an impoverished young gentlewoman.

As for the two principals involved, they were quite busy with shopping and planning for the journey—and with each other—that no word of the scandal abuilding reached their ears.

When all had been done that had to be done and they were about to set out for Bath, a disappointment lay in store for at least two of the party. Mary, for her part, was thankful for the respite. They did set out, but not with the marquis. A message had come for him at the last minute which forced him to excuse himself and permit the small cavalcade to begin the hundred-mile trip without him.

❧

The Duchess of Verndon looked with some annoyance at the *Journal* spread out like a curtain across the breakfast table.

"Steven, please put the newspaper down! For one, I think I have quite forgot what you look like and would refresh my memory. For another, I wish to discuss your son. I have had the most disheartening news."

His Grace lowered the paper and displayed a countenance, which except for the beaming grin which disfigured it, must have been one of great dignity.

"You have a most endearing quality about you, m'love. Your use of hyperbole is scandalous. I believe you saw me quite well this morning when—"

"Steven!!" cried the little duchess. "Have a care what you say! The servants!"

He chuckled. "Let that be a lesson to you, my dear. *I* have no need of extravagant exaggeration to gain *your* attention."

"Oh, you and your odious son are cut from the same cloth!"

"Quite. I have high hopes for the boy, therefore."

"But he is nigh on to thirty years of age! I should think it high time he gave over this-this debauchery of his and became respectable."

"After he has sown his oats—"

"Oh, you keep saying that every time he is brought up!"

"Then why don't *you* speak to him. He never listens to *me!*"

"You are his father and he is your son—"

"Now, Elvira, you say that as if I was the sole prepetrator. Do not put it all on me! I distinctly recall you had as much to do with his being brought into this world as I did if not a deal more! I am not exactly sure when it was, but to the best of my recollection—"

"Steven, if you persist in going on in such an odious fashion, I shall leave the table!"

"You know, my love, you are definitely not my idea of a duchess, and when your eyes sparkle with anger—Gad! What a mistress you might have made me!"

Her Grace regarded her great husband with a knowing smile. "It did almost come to that. You were so enamored of that blond Windford woman that if I had not seduced you, heaven knows what a chase she'd have led you."

"What? You seduced me! The devil you say! It was quite the other way around I assure you!"

"Was it truly? Hah! I remember it well! After it was over you brought me home and did not even kiss me! As for saying you loved me, nothing was further from your mind. I cried all that night into my pillow."

There was a mixture of pain and tenderness on

His Grace's face as he nodded and reached across the table to take possession of her hand.

"I shall never come to understand why you deigned to marry such a noodle as I was, but I thank all of heaven that you did. I hope you have not been too disappointed."

She squeezed his hand and smiled. "No, Your Grace, I have not been too disappointed."

He withdrew his hand and reached for the newspaper.

"Steven!"

He forgot the newspaper and laughed. "Gad, I thought I had got your mind off the subject. You are no bigger than a gnat and twice as persistent!"

"How very flattering of you to say so, Your Grace. What about Anthony?"

"Wildest colts make the best horses!"

"Steven!"

The large nobleman sighed. "Very well, I shall speak with him again."

"At once, Steven. His latest escapade bids fair to bring shame upon our house."

"Oh?"

"You should have taken him in hand long before this—"

"Elvira, enough! You have made vile accusation against our son. I would know your grounds."

"I have had word from more quarters than I care to mention. He is seeing a young gentlewoman, one whose circumstances are so reduced that she must needs keep a shop, a bookshop in Bloomsbury. She has no family to protect her except a female cousin little older than herself. You know as well as I do there can be but one outcome."

"I do not like this one bit!" His Grace looked stern.

"I hold no brief for the girl. I daresay she is as good as she would be, but how must it look for Montreat to bring to ruination such a vulnerable prey."

"You are quite right, my dear. This must not go further. I shall send an express to Tony first thing to call upon me."

"Thank you, Steven, and see if you cannot turn his mind to a more serious and laudable ambition."

"Never fear. He has gone far enough—too far, in fact. It is high time he came to behave like a future Duke of Verndon."

ཐ

The note to the Marquis of Montreat was in effect a summons and from a personage for whom Tony had great love and respect. It was not a request he could disregard in the least and so he had to bid Beth farewell for a time, promising that he would be in Bath as soon as he possibly could.

He did not note the disappointment in her eyes, nor how she anxiously awaited his promise to come out, for he was too occupied in his mind trying to determine what it was his father wished to see him about. The duke and he had always been on the best of terms. His physical resemblance to his father had never been great. They were of about equal stature but the duke was a broad man and fair whereas the marquis was dark, like his mother, and had inherited her fine lineaments. But, as to character, and deportment, he and his sire were so alike that there was an empathy between them rarely seen between two men, however close.

Without delay, he had his curricle brought out and prepared to make a rapid descent into Kent.

Sevenoaks was less than a half-day's drive out of London for a crack whip driving such a pair of flyers and, as it took the marquis well out of his way to Bath, he was at pains to cover the ground quickly, which he did in record time. It was at some cost to himself and his beasts that he arrived at his destination.

Oaklands, the Quarnell family seat, consisted of a massive manor house, a substantial edifice in the rubbed and finely jointed brickwork of the Wren tradition, set in a park, richly wooded with great oaks. The size and age of the trees, considering the recency of the building—it had been standing less than a hundred years—attested to the great wealth that the family had already amassed when William and Mary ascended the throne, because it was obvious that the trees had never sprouted naturally in the artful arrangement but had had to be uprooted and transplanted to make the oaken park what it had become.

The marquis never returned to Oaklands without feeling a nostalgic wrench. He had spent so much of his childhood there, even attending the nearby Sevenoaks boys school as a day scholar before going up to Oxford. But the fact that his charming parents were rarely absent from the place for long was its greatest attraction for him.

Normally he would have stopped to chat with old Hillary, the ancient groundsman who lived at the gate lodge, but he was in a tearing rush to see His Grace and get back to the business he had in hand, so he bowled on through the arched gateway with only a hail for the old retainer.

He knew something quite serious was in the wind for, as he pulled up by the entrance front, there was the tall, sturdy figure of his father, his iron-gray locks somewhat whiter since last they had met, coming out to greet him.

He leaped from the curricle and strode forward with his hand outstretched. The duke came to meet him and shook hands with him vigorously as he placed his arm about Tony's shoulders.

"Tony, it is good to see you, lad! I could wish it was not so very long between your visits. You come in good time, for I had just sent you an express to call."

"I know, Your Grace. That is why I have come."

The duke looked his surprise as they entered the house.

"You say you have received my note?" he asked incredulously.

"Yes, sir."

"Blast me! You must have grown wings since I saw you last."

The marquis laughed. "No, I have not grown wings, but as I have an iron in the fire and in need of tending, I thought to make this visit a quick one. I wish to be in Bath by the weekend."

His Grace frowned. "Well, do not count on it. We have matters of grave import to discuss. There is some port in the library, and I think it best we get to it without delay. Hah! The port and the business," he added with a chuckle.

"Your Grace, look at me! I am dust and mud from head to foot. I'd have made better time were it not for the accursed weather. Drenching downpours ambushed me at every turn. By your leave, I should like to change and freshen up a bit—and, of course, pay my respects to Her Grace. How is our little darling?"

"Quite well and as anxious to see you as ever. But she will defer her pleasure until you and I have had a chat." He examined the travel-stained appearance of his son. "Yes, you had best go to your room. You are in a sorry state. I'll send Gates to you. After, come to me in the library. I shall be awaiting you."

"Very good, Your Grace. I shan't be long. Allow me some thirty minutes."

ॐ

"Well!" exclaimed the duke, nodding his head in approval as his son, looking clean and neat, made his appearance. "You are a devilishly handsome fellow, Tony! Though I doubt that I am telling you something you were not well aware of—but why, in God's creation, you must wear that infernal black I cannot begin to surmise! Damme if you do not look a mourner for hire!"

"It is quite an effective mode of dress. They *will* call me 'Rakehell' and I *will* show them myself covered with soot to fit the appellation."

"Pfah! You look a damned sweep! Damned childish conceit! Here, pour yourself a glass and let us get down to the reckoning, for you have an account to render to me."

Tony regarded his father in wonder. "Your Grace, I cannot think what you are driving at."

"Then I shall tell you. By the way, what do you think of the port? A rare vintage; '78 y'know!"

"Mmm-mm! Excellent! Could you spare me a bottle or two?" asked Tony, holding his glass up and peering into its deep ruby depths.

"I have got me two dozen, half of which I have had set aside for you. Good thing you came when you did. I'd not have let them sit idle if *my* stock ran out."

Tony smiled and said: "Thank you, Father."

"Now then, Sevenoaks is well out of the heart of things but, sooner or later, word of your activities reaches us here. I have always held that you be permitted to do as you list, for I am a man who belives that the fires of youth require a great deal of tempering, not quenching. But, of late, my patience has grown thin, for you are hardly a youth any longer. Your persistence in making a name for yourself, one that I can take no pride in at all, forces me to speak. 'Rakehell,' indeed! Your mother has never cared for this foul reputation you have garnered, and I have been at pains to console her with the thought that it is to be expected and is only a temporary thing. But this latest escapade is too much— if it *is* your latest and not past history by this time.

In light of it, I can no longer in good conscience stand between you and Her Grace's disapproval. I must request you change your ways at once!"

Tony was frowning as his father finished his declaration and demand.

"Your Grace, with all due respect, I must inform you that the gossip has been blown out of all proportion. Yes, it is quite true I have had a fair number of connexions—"

"A fair number? Indeed, I have lost count!"

"Well, it is hardly of any consequence. I have done no one harm. The ladies have been, shall we say, kind to me, and my time has been occupied—er—attempting to placate them. I cannot say that I have been all that content with matters, but what is one to do when one is bored!"

"Marry and settle down! A good wife will see to it that you are not bored. I speak from experience!"

Tony chuckled. "I daresay you do, and for the longest time I was without hope that I should ever be as fortunate, but that is over now. I have at long last discovered a young lady who, though she believes me to be the embodiment of evil, is not afraid to deal with me."

"Deal? I never knew you to be so mealymouthed with words before."

"Yes, deal! I have a business arrangement with her."

His Grace looked disgusted. "Very well, you

have a *business* arrangement with her. We called it 'mounting a mistress' in my day. Then this business with the Brown girl is over and done with? I hope you covered your indiscretion with her?"

"She is not my mistress, and it is not over and done with by far! It is a *business* arrangement we have got between us, and it is a *business* arrangement I mean!"

"Do not fly off at me, Tony, and I'll thank you not to lie! I am not one of your bosom admirers who can see no wrong in you!"

"But, Your Grace—"

"Silence! We have had it on very good authority that the Brown woman is as poor as a church mouse, a gentlewoman who must eke out her independence by keeping a bookshop—"

"The bookshop is all she has, she and her cousin. She has no independence."

"Then it is even worse than I thought. There can only be one sort of business arrangement between a wealthy nobleman and such as she. What a blot upon the Quarnell escutcheon, to lead astray an unprotected English gentlewoman! I'll not have it, sir!"

Tony glared at his father. His face was pale and his eyes glowed like living coals.

In a voice hoarse with emotion, he declared: "Your Grace, if I could have seduced Elizabeth Brown, I should have. I tried and I failed."

"Nonsense! Do you expect me to believe such twaddle? When have you ever failed in such an enterprise?"

"Never, my lord, until I came to meet up with Miss Brown. But I have not given up. One way or another I shall have her. If it is the last thing I ever do, I shall have her!"

"You dare to say so to my face?! Do you realize the scandal you will bring down upon our heads? Do you realize that if you persist in this transgression against all that society holds sacred, you become an outcast. Why, dammit all, you will wind up having to marry the girl!"

To His Grace's great surprise and indignation, his son burst out laughing.

"My lord, you are impudent!" thundered His Grace.

"I beg you, Father, disabuse yourself of the thought. You know I could never be so to you. What you have said is humorous to me and when you come to know Beth, you will appreciate it."

"That is outside of enough—"

"Your Grace, I wish you would show less indignation and pay more attention. We have never been so out in our thinking as we are at this moment. Perhaps it is because I got off on the wrong foot with Beth, in fact, I am sure it is, but she has taken a dislike to my manner—I pray it is only that and nothing more. Yes, I thought to make an easy conquest of her. The very first moment I saw her I knew I must have her and—out of my insufferable conceit—completely misjudged the girl. I could not win her to my bed for any consideration—no, not even marriage!"

"You did not offer for her?" exclaimed His Grace aghast.

"Aye, and received a fair setdown for my pains."

"For heaven's sake, how long has this been going on?"

Tony laughed. "I have known her for something less than a fortnight, but she dealt me a proper dusting within minutes of my first laying eyes upon her."

The duke looked at his son very disapprovingly. "You have gone too far. I see I shall have to take a strong hand with you. Beauty is not everything. There is a deal more to a woman, one with whom you would wish to cast your lot with for the rest of your years, than comeliness of person."

"Beth is not in the least a beauty," retorted Tony.

"Then I do not understand you at all! You offered for this person upon your first meeting with her—I'll not comment further upon that at this time—for no reason in the world that I can see. She is no beauty, she is dreadfully poor, a name of Brown—Beth Brown, at that—which means her breeding, provided she has any at all, is insignificant as compared to your own—and she is in trade!"

Tony fired back at him. "Now, Your Grace, you may deem me impudent and I do not care, but I have heard tell of a gentlewoman of a small independence, the daughter of a less than affluent baronet who perforce had turned to trade. He was in grain if I have it correctly. She married a duke and her name was Smith!"

At that His Grace turned purple. "You dare!" he cried.

"You have forced me!" declared Tony. "Lady Elvira Smith, now Her Grace, the Duchess of Verndon and my adored and respected mother, was as far beneath a duke when you wed her as my Beth is beneath a marquis, now!"

"My lords, must you shout so! I do declare, Steven, that is not any proper way to conduct a discussion with your son. And you, Tony, don't you dare to take that tone of voice with your father! This is not the House of *Commons*, my *lords!*" scolded Lady Elvira as she came into the room.

There was an immediate halt in the hostilities as both husband and son abruptly came to their feet, their faces softening into smiles.

"Mother, you look as charming as ever!" declared Tony with a delighted grin as he came over, lifted her up in his arms, deposited a loud smack upon her smooth cheek and set her down again.

She chortled a bit and patted at her hair while she said: "Tony, I know you are quite large and marvelously strong. I do not need a demonstration each time you call. A tender salute upon the cheek will serve as well." She turned to Duke Steven. "My lord, what is going forward? I can not help but be curious when so much tumult is engendered."

"Your son, madam—"

"Father, I beg leave to plead my own cause."

The duke shrugged. "Very well, for I am hanged if I understand!"

Tony turned to his mother. "It is simply this, my lady. The rumors concerning me that have reached your ears in the past were probably all quite true—if somewhat exaggerated. I have not been an angel and I have not pretended to be. But this last gossip which has Father high up in the trees is completely false."

"This Miss Brown is not the object of your attention?"

"Well, yes she is, but not in the way you think!"

"And how do I think, my son?"

Tony's face turned beet red. "Oh, I say, Mother, that is not a fair question. You know what I mean."

Lady Elvira smiled. "What would you *have* me think?"

"I would have you think that Miss Brown is a gentlewoman, uncorrupted by me and incorruptble."

"She's as poor as a peasant, Elvira!" interjected Lord Steven.

"She is in trade, is she not?" asked the duchess calmly.

"Yes, a bookseller."

Lady Elvira's left eyebrow shot up. "Exactly what is your interest in her?"

"I want her!"

"Son, you may not have every female you fancy, and I fear Miss Brown is one of them. It would be the most odious thing you could do, to bring ruin to a young gentlewoman, especially as she has no family, as I have heard tell. Leave her be and find your amusement in quarters where it will do no harm—and *that* is something I wish to speak to you about."

"Mother, you do not understand!"

"I understand well enough to know that your gadding about from flower to flower must come to an end. You are already a disgrace to your name, and your father has had his fill of it. You had best begin to consider seriously some female of impeccable reputation for your consort—although what fine young lady will welcome your attention, I do not know."

Tony pursed his lips and regarded his mother while he appeared to ponder her remarks.

"By heaven, I think you have put me on the right track. Of course! It has got to be marriage!" and he burst into happy laughter.

"Well, I am relieved that you find the prospect a

cheerful one! What I shall do—if you promise to behave yourself with all due respect and decorum—is to look about and see if I cannot put you next to some young lady. We have an excellent group of maidens here in our own neighborhood—"

"No, no. There is no need! I have already found her! It is just that I have not gone about it the right way."

"Who have you found?"

"Beth Brown."

"Beth!—Oh, this Elizabeth Brown. That is not what I had in mind, Tony! For shame! You would never marry your mistress!"

"Curse all those wagging tongues that have so poisoned your minds against her!" cried Tony.

The duke got to his feet in high indignation. "Anthony, cease these histrionics at once! What sort of behavior is this—and before your mother, too!"

Tony shook his head and bowed to Lady Elvira. "Your Grace, a thousand pardons! But I am irked beyond bearing that you should have been so grossly misled."

"Misled, my Lord Rakehell?!" demanded the duke vehemently.

Tony stood his ground and wheeled to face his father.

"Your Grace, I beg leave to speak before this confounded and confused business gets tangled further."

"You have talked and you have talked and, as yet, have said nothing to any effect. After all, what is there left for you to say?"

"Simply this. I have said it before, but you did not listen. Miss Elizabeth Brown is not my mistress! Nor has she ever been!"

Lady Elvira looked at her son and her eyes were sad. "Tony, this is not good in you, and I shall hold it against this Brown person. You have never lied to us before. I am sorely disappointed."

"Mother, I have told you the truth."

Lady Elvira sighed. "From unimpeachable sources, I have been informed that you were seen with this person in more than one of the best shops in London."

"I do not deny it. She had to purchase a wardrobe."

"In the best shops, and she so poor?"

"They are the only shops at which I have accounts," he replied in all seriousness.

Lady Elvira gazed at him, the hint of a smile upon her lips.

He rushed to qualify his answer. "I assure you, Your Grace, she is to pay for her purchases. I was along to vouch for her credit."

"Lame, Tony, lame!" said the duke. "You will have to do better than that!"

"Yes, my son, for it will not wash. Since she is poor, she can have no credit, other than your word.

There is no money; therefore, as you have vouched for her, it will be you who finally settles her bills. How can you ask us to believe then that she is not your mistress?"

"She will pay for it all. She has not the money now, but she has got a commission and will have ample funds upon its completion."

"What sort of commission?" demanded Lord Steven.

"Why-er-ah-she has qualification to be an antiquarian and has been employed to examine an estate." Tony was beginning to feel very uncomfortable, and the fact was obvious to his parents as he eased his neckband.

"Fiddlesticks and poppycock!" expostulated Lord Steven. "She could not earn enough in a year to pay for one single gown from Charmelle's or Dickerson's or any of that lot!"

Tony smiled ruefully. "I see that I am only making matters worse."

"Is it not always the way when one is deceitful?" asked the duchess.

"It appears to be just as difficult when one is not! I must ask your patience, for I see I shall have to tell you the entire story from the beginning. It is the only way you shall ever have the right of it—and now, for me, it is most important that you do understand."

Lady Elvira smiled approvingly. "Yes, Tony, I

think it is time you stopped trying to hide whatever it is you are hiding. In any case, I must admit to an abiding curiosity concerning your progress in the courts of Eros. I hope your hints that it will be a love story prove true, for I dearly love a romance."

"You'll not be disappointed, I assure you."

Duke Steven grumbled: "I hardly think the adventures of a rake, be he the Marquis of Montreat or no, a fit topic for chaste ears."

"Oh, do be still, Steven! What is the fun of having a rackety libertine for a son and not gain some diversion from his pursuits? We may not approve but, at least, we can listen."

"I say, is that any proper way to speak of your own son?" protested Tony.

Lady Elvira retorted: "Of course it is not, and I beg your pardon, Tony. But it is just that propriety forbids me the use of language more appropriate."

His Grace let out a guffaw, and Tony looked sheepish.

"I guess I deserve that," he admitted, "but let me tell you of this latest, and perhaps you will see some small cause to amend your opinion.

"As you know, Uncle Ethelbert's estate near Bath came to me and, of course, I had no use for it. I imagine the old boy had no great liking for me and saddled me with it for spite."

Lord Steven interposed. "No, Tony, that is not so. It is sad that Ethelbert became so ingrown to the extent that he found it necessary to adopt that surly facade; but, in actual fact, lad, you were the son he could never have once he had renounced the world and given himself over to his avocation of collecting parchments. Even now, it is painful for your mother and I to discuss it, but, in a sense, we owe it to his memory to acquaint you with the facts. Your uncle was my stepbrother, as you know, and to say that there was bad blood between us is to put it too strongly, for we were very close in our younger years.

"It was the blow your mother dealt him when she rejected his suit and accepted mine that caused the rift and turned him into the poor excuse of a man you knew him as. He held it against me that I was the first-born, and he convinced himself that your mother was influenced by my inheritance in making her choice.

"As a result he elected to resign from the world. I daresay, had he been of a papist conviction, he'd have turned monk. As it was, I gave him outright the house and lands of Gryfynskepe, which he chose himself for his residence, and settled an independence upon him. That he saw fit to bequeath it all to you speaks eloquently of his continued devotion to Her Grace, your mother."

There was pain in Tony's eyes. "But why was I never told of this?"

"Because he made it quite clear that he wanted no

reminder of the past. The sight of you could have only discomfited him, and he was content to indulge his eccentricity in solitude."

"I owe the old gentleman an apology."

"Do not let it worry you, dear," said the duchess. "I am sure this is the way he wished things to be. Now, go on with your tale."

"Yes, well, where was I? Oh yes! What I saw when I visited the place did not tempt me to retain it, and I came back to London resolved upon its disposal. The building had been so poorly maintained it was worth next to nothing, for it would cost as much as it was worth to redecorate it in any reasonable style; but the land, because of its proximity to Bath, should have brought in some few thousand pounds. You can imagine my surprise when, within days of my having had it listed, I received an offer of £14,000. It gave me to think that something was rotten in the state of Denmark. Since I was satisfied of the value of the place, I could only conclude that it must be something other than the land or the buildings that could account for such an exorbitant bid. Other than Uncle Ethelbert's bizarre accumulations, I could not think of any reason. I consulted with our solicitor, and he mentioned a Charles Brown, a book vendor, of whom he had heard as having expertise in antiquities, especially documents—"

"Why the devil did you not think to come to

me?" demanded His Grace. "I, too, have some expertise in that direction, you know!"

"Well really, Father, I'd hardly expect you to go out to Bath and rummage through stacks and stacks of musty old parchment."

The duke grunted an unwilling agreement. "I could have put you in touch with a good man. I do not recall any Charles Brown in connection with such studies."

Impatiently, Lady Elvira declared: "You can argue about Mr. Brown's qualifications later. It is in his daughter's that I am interested."

"Yes, of course. The beggar's dead anyway," remarked the duke.

Tony continued: "I repaired to the shop and—well, that is where it all started. There was this young woman tending it, and I stated my business to her, handing her my card. Her response was not insolent—at least, not upon the surface—but I had no doubt that she was taking pains to make a mock of me. I could not believe I had heard aright and exerted myself to put her in her place. The result was she gave me quite a thorough trimming and made me aware that I was dealing with a person who held me in contempt and did not fear to express herself on that point. Immediately I set myself to win her over. In fact, she had piqued my interest to such an extent that I determined to gain my end with her."

"You mean she challenged your pride in your address with females, and you could not bear it," commented Lady Elvira.

"You need not be so blunt about it, Your Grace," said Tony with a laugh. "But I'll not say you are wrong. I offered her *carte blanche* and she turned it aside—not with great shock, mind you, but in a manner that left me in no doubt that she was not being coy with me. I'll never forget what she said. 'All I have is this shop and my reputation. You would deprive me of both.' I assured her that I would make it worth her while, and she responded most amazingly. She asked me why I did not offer her marriage if I was willing to go to such expense as it would be a deal cheaper!"

"She didn't!" exclaimed His Grace.

"Go on, Tony," said Her Grace impatiently.

"You know, that brought me up sharply. I studied her as I thought about it. I was suddenly aware that I wanted her more than anything else in the world. There was that about her, standing up to me so forthright, dealing with me on equal footing, that I accepted the proposition and made my offer on the spot!"

"Great God in heaven!" exclaimed Duke Steven.

Lady Elvira quieted her husband with a gesture and stated: "This Miss Brown must be a beautiful creature to have affected you so."

"No, my lady, Beth is not what one would call

beautiful. She is neat and fresh in appearance and not unpleasant to look at, but no one would take her for a great beauty—but that is not to say she is unattractive. There is an air about her that—well, I do not know how to describe it, but—it warms me to look upon her and listen to her. I cannot say more.

Well, to make a long story short, I offered her the commission—because she had succeeded her father—I offered her *carte blanche*, I offered her marriage, and she rejected each and every one of my proposals. I felt so—so frustrated with her and I grew so angry at her intransigence that"—he paused to mop his brow—"I am very ashamed and embarrassed to relate to you what followed. I would not do so except that it is you to whom I am revealing it, and I would have you know the full extent of what lies behind my obligation to Miss Brown.

"It was a new experience for me to be thwarted so, especially by one of such low station and obvious poverty, and I took it as an affront. I thought to teach her a lesson and threatened to possess her right there and then. I even went so far as to bolt the door and cover the window." He paused, overwrought by his recollection.

"Son, it was a very poor jest!" remarked the duchess. "Really, I am ashamed of you for even feigning to be so base."

"Let me proceed. It gets worse."

"You mean to say—!" chorused the duke and duchess together.

"I pray you will let me proceed. No, it never got *that* bad!"

"Go on, Anthony. I am liking this recitation less and less with each passing moment," declared Lady Elvira.

His Grace appeared to be having difficulty restraining himself.

"I came towards her, ignoring her pleas—and it is at this point I break into a sweat every time I think of it—I do not know what would have occurred if she had not swooned. But thank heaven, she did! It gave me such a blow to my heart that I came to my senses in an instant. I nursed her back to consciousness with a sip of brandy that almost choked her. I can tell you that when I saw the panic in her eyes, and the disdain, I feared that I had committed a piece of foolishness that I might live to regret to the end of my days. It was clear to me as I held her in my arms that I must have her or I should never know happiness again."

"How much did it take to quiet her?" asked the duke.

For a moment Tony could not make out what it was the duke was asking. Then his brow cleared as he understood. "Ah, you mean money! Let me assure you, Your Grace, she made no claim. I offered her my wallet, and it saddened me to understand how truly poor she was, because even as she refused it, she must needs put her hands behind her to resist the temptation."

Lady Elvira frowned.

Tony went on: "When I think of it, I must be more solicitous of Uncle Ethelbert's memory than ever. For, if it had not been for the errand I had, I'd have lost her then. I think I convinced her that it was all meant as an unseemly jest and then proceeded to haggle with her over the conditions under which she would accept my commission."

"But you did convince her," said the duchess, "and I daresay at a handsome fee."

Tony chuckled. "You make it sound as though she were the eager one. On the contrary, Mother, never have I had to work so long and so hard to convince a female of my sincerity, and this was probably the only time I ever truly was. And as to the fee, she recommended other, more experienced experts than herself and finally informed me that she might have to charge me as much as thirty-five pounds if the examination required more than a month's time. I tell you I was at my wit's end how to keep her interest without straining her credibility. She brought up all the sorts of expenses that must be incurred on a visit to Gryfynskepe, and I declared they were all quite legitimate and should be charged against me, her employer—which of course they are not. To seal the bargain, I insisted she accept my wallet as an advance against the trip and dine with me at Claridge's. That, too, became a subject for debate, but finally she accepted. I still had not learned my lesson and was no angel with her, but she set me down with a thump and, after that, we got on much better.

"I helped her shop for the things she required and informed the various proprietors that, although they were to render the bills to her, I would be good for them. I suppose that is what gave the gossip the twist I had hoped to avoid by making my appearance with her Claridge's.

"We were just leaving for Bath when your summons arrived. I sent her off secure in the knowledge that I had a string on her—a string of debt some thirteen hundred and fifty pounds in length—a sum of which I am sure she is not aware."

"Since she cannot possibly repay such a sum, exactly what do you expect of her when she is asked to settle her accounts?" His Grace wished to know.

"Whatever I may hope for, from the Marquise of Montreat."

"You speak of marriage, and you do not even know that she is a gentlewoman for sure! You have only her word for that. And she is a shopkeeper!!"

"Please, my lord, not so loud!" cautioned Lady Elvira. "Tony—and what if this Miss Brown has no affection for you—I could hardly blame her if she did not—what then?"

"At the moment she does not dislike me. I have recouped much of the ground lost by my unconscionable behavior."

"You do not respond to my question. I see you are weaving a web and would force her to wed you. Suppose that she will not. What then?"

Tony shrugged and with a sickly smile, said: "Then I shall have lost some £1,350 and so much more, I do not care to think on it."

"I have listened to you carefully, and from all you have seen fit to tell us, I am left in grave doubt as to the character of this person. It strikes me that Miss Brown may be an extremely clever sort—"

"You have my word, she most certainly is!"

"—and is about to lighten your pockets to an exceptionable degree."

"Mother, I owe her that opportunity. But I do not believe she is anything like that."

"Well, I am not so sure. But, tell me, why do you not offer for her again, now that she must understand fully the extent of your wealth and the high station she would be accorded as your wife?"

"Elvira, how dare you suggest anything of the sort!" protested His Grace.

"My lord, I am trying to come to some conclusions about your son and about Miss Elizabeth Brown."

"I shall save you the trouble as I have already

reached my own. Allow me to handle this, my dear."

He addressed his son: "Tony, what you do with this person, I care not a whit; but this talk of marriage is utter nonsense and, as head of the Quarnell family, I forbid it."

"Steven, that was not at all what I had in mind! Now, look what you have done to the boy!"

Tony was standing quite rigid, his lips tightly pressed together as if he dared not trust himself to speak for fear of what he might say.

"But how can I say less?" appealed the duke to his wife. "We do not know anything about her—and Tony has known her, by his own admission, less than a fortnight."

"What has that to say to anything? Will you allow me to proceed in this matter in my own way, my lord?"

"Yes, if you insist. But it all seems quite clear to me."

"I bow to your superior insight, my lord, and beg you to have patience with me until I can see it all as clearly."

The duke turned to his son. "I daresay you can be at ease, lad. The true head of the Quarnell family has just granted you a reprieve."

Tony could not help smiling. "Thank you, my lady."

"I would have an answer to my question, still. Why do you not repeat your offer to her now?"

"For a number of reasons. First of all, she will not take me seriously if I did. Secondly, I am enjoying her company as I have never enjoyed that of any other female and am loath to do anything to jeopardize the present arrangement. And third—" he hesitated.

"And third?"

"It is very ungallant of me, I know, to rashly proclaim my love for her one minute and then the very next to say that I have a reservation. I wonder at her willingness to accept, now, all that I offer. I do not begrudge one penny of the funds that I have committed to her benefit, for, all things aside, it is small recompense for what I put her through; but she is a woman of business. The shop has been in her keeping four years now, and she did not come to it green, having been under her father's tutelage up until his death. There is a possibility you are right in your suspicions, my lady, and I suppose that I shall have to pay for the privilege of finding out. Certainly, I cannot walk away from her now!"

"I should think not!" declared the duke. "That's a handsome bit of brass you've got invested!"

"Steven, I pray you will not be so crass! That is not at all pertinent!" scolded Lady Elvira.

She turned to Tony. "Son, when you are satisfied, bring her here to us at Oaklands."

"And how say you, Your Grace?" asked Tony of his father.

The duke grinned. "Your gesture, dear boy, is appreciated, but I am no match for your mother when it comes to affairs of the heart and well she knows it. If you wish it, Miss Brown will be welcome here. I understand now what your mother was driving at, and I see I did not have as clear an understanding of you as I thought. Now, perhaps we can get off this trying topic onto something more pleasant. How did that race between young Benton and Scofield turn out. . . ?"

Although Tony was quite anxious to get away, it was inconceivable that, having been absent some three months from Oaklands, he could leave earlier than two days. Under ordinary circumstances he would have been glad to do so, spend a week with his parents even, but he could not keep his mind off Bath—more specifically what Beth was doing there, how she was spending her time.

On the morning of the third day, he took leave of their Graces, got into his curricle and went dashing down the lane. Now that he was finally on his way, he was more anxious than ever. Before he had ever passed through the gateway of the estate, he had got his beasts moving at a goodly clip. He was bound and determined to be in Bath by the weekend.

ॐ

The cavalcade to Bath was comprised of two vehicles: a cumbersome traveling coach behind, in which were two lady's maids and a cook, together with luggage completely filling the boot and overflowing onto the roof, and a light softly sprung coach ahead, in which were Beth and Mary.

One of the drivers was the marquis' very own coachman, and perched up in the driving seat of the second carriage was an assistant groom of some experience and a deal more ambition, having a hope to succeed the coachman. There were ten horses along; two pairs drawing each vehicle, a lady's saddle horse from my lord's stables trailing, while the tenth horse was in the lead mounted by Cowles.

Cowles was master of the train and was taking his role quite seriously. He rode a cavalry saddle and wore a cavalry saber. In his belt was a formidable horse pistol and a wicked-looking boarding blunderbuss was at hand in his saddle boot. His tall, well-armed figure must have given pause to more than one highwayman along the way, who might otherwise have considered the carriages ripe plums for the picking.

At some point along the line of travel, Mary remarked: "Beth, I do not feel at all well—"

"Oh, dear God in heaven above, I hope you are not coming down with a fever!" exclaimed Beth reaching for her cousin's hand.

Mary smiled and shook her head. "No, it is not anything like that. I refer to a feeling of foreboding that has haunted me ever since his lordship saw fit to abandon us at the last minute."

"I do not see anything to be upset about. I daresay he has other concerns that may take precedence over the business we are engaged in."

"What did he say to you?"

"That he was suddenly called away to see some people who are of very great importance to him and that he might be expected in Bath by the weekend."

Mary shook her head. "I do not trust him. I'd not put it past him to ride on ahead to prepare some foul plot so as to catch you off your guard."

"My dear Mary, Lord Quarnell has no need to extend himself to that end. He has got me at a disadvantage already. It was quite difficult to keep account, what with my eyes so bedazzled by all the exquisite finery we purchased; but, as best as I can remember, I am sure that I have spent well over £1,200 and not a penny of it earned."

"But you could not have!" protested Mary. "Why that is a fortune! You could not repay it in a lifetime."

"Yes, I know. But what was I to do? I had gone as far as I could to deal with him. If I was not to lose him so soon, short of abject surrender, I had to go along with his exorbitant idea of what are legitimate expenses. If I had not, I am sure I should have lost his interest, and he would have gone off and forgotten all about me. It seemed the only way! I only hope and pray that these people of great importance are not some other female."

"Oh, Beth, what are you saying? I think you have quite lost your wits over the gentleman—and your wits are what you shall need most to face what must befall you."

"Well, we shall know the worst when we arrive at Gryfynskepe. If it should turn out to be a delightful bower with nary a hint of those mythical rooms filled with antique documents, we shall know it is truly my Lord Rakehell we have to contend with." She chuckled. "Of course, even if Gryfyneskepe should turn out to be as he described it, that is not to say all will be well. I'd not put it past him to go to any length in what he is so quick to refer to as one of his jests."

"Beth, it is still not too late. Let us go back. You

can return all the pretty things and give over this folly of a commission. Then there will be no doubt, and his lordship cannot fail to understand your determination to see no more of him."

"Mary, for one thing, I have no such determination. For another, what must the world be made to think of my Lord Marquis if I were to do such a thing? I should make him look so great a fool as I could never bear to look him in the face again."

"And what sort of fool shall *you* be made to look if you go on with this madness?"

Beth shrugged. "Nothing so exceptional. I shall just become another one of a great company, not worthy of particular remark. But let us talk of something else. 'Sufficient unto the day is the evil thereof' is, in this case, the best advice."

Silence reigned between them for a while as the carriage rolled on. The rumble of the wheels and the creaking of the leather springs were the only sounds to be heard within the luxurious, leather-upholstered interior.

Mary, looking out of the window, remarked: "That Mr. Cowles is a very interesting person."

"The footman or whatever?"

"He is not any footman! I believe he is high in the confidence of the marquis. I have heard tell he was a major in the 17th Lancers and left it for service with his lordship."

"An officer reduced to being a servant? How shocking!"

"No, no," Mary assured her, "he was not an officer! But he was no ordinary soldier either."

"But you said he was a major."

"Well, a major—something. I forget which, but I did not understand he had been an officer."

Beth laughed. "I do not suppose you mean to say he was a *sergeant* major?"

"Yes, that is what he said—a sergeant major."

Beth regarded her cousin with curiosity. "You have spoken with him?"

Mary smiled abashedly and blushed. "One cannot help but converse, when one is seeing to the packing and things with one, can one?"

Beth smiled. "He does not look anything at all like a servant now. It explains why my lord entrusted our funds to him. I wondered at the time."

"Yes, he can put his hand to anything and is not exactly a servant to the marquis, more like a—a king has! You know, if the marquis were a king, then he would be Sir Joshua Cowles because of his connection and not because of his birth particularly."

"A man-at-arms sort of thing?"

"Yes."

"Well, my dear cousin, I caution you to beware. It could well be a case of like master, like man."

"Oh, I do not think Joshua is anything like his lordship! I am sure he is most trustworthy."

"Do I detect a warmer note than mere friendliness already exists between you?"

"Oh, Beth, if you make fun of me, I shall die!"

"My dearest Mary, who am I to make a mock of your affections? If you are losing your heart to Joshua Cowles, and he is what he seems, how much more fortunate—and wiser—are you than I!"

❦

"Oh dear, I can see now why it is called 'Gryfynskepe'!" exclaimed Beth as a low, massive building came into view. "Surely it is the relict of some ancient castle, which someone had the poor taste to decorate with grotesque wings and heads as makes it appear about to launch itself into flight. What a monstrosity!"

Mary declared: "I shudder to think of the time we must spend within those forbidding and undoubtedly musty precincts. I am almost hoping there are no rooms of parchments."

"I quite agree. Suddenly, I am relieved to know that your Mr. Cowles is along with us. What it must be like within, I fear to surmise."

As they drew nearer, they could discern a small group of laborers at work on the high road where the lane from Gryfynskepe joined it.

"They were better employed upon the building than the road," commented Beth.

Neither of them was particularly pleased to see that the old keep was situated upon a short but steep rise so that the lane could not approach it directly but had to go round about before it ever got to the front door. The outbuildings, of which there were two, were in even sadder shape, and it must have been apparent to the least informed that their half score of horses would barely find shelter in them, to say nothing of the two equipages.

Suddenly Beth burst into elated glee. "You will admit," she said with a chortle, "that the marquis could not have selected a worse place if he had anything but business on his mind. Now, if he had been contemplating a murder, I daresay he could not have selected a better."

The party wended its way up the circuitous approach and finally came to a halt upon the paved floor of what had been some part of a courtyard in the dim past. As though to impress them more deeply with the grim-looking edifice, the sun slipped behind a great cloud bank and gusts of dampish wind began to tug at their skirts.

Beth experienced a chill and its intensity was more than the turbulent air could account for.

"What an odious place!" she exclaimed. "The Castle of Otranto must have been a veritable Eden by comparison. If there are no more but two specters within, I shall be astounded. Let us hope the builder relented and made adequate compensation within for the outrage in taste he committed without. Br-r-r! It has suddenly gone quite chilly. I do hope there is a cozy fire within."

The great portal swung open and a stocky, snub-nosed man, followed by a tall, hunched-over woman, came out.

Beth whispered aside to Mary: "Our worst fears are more than realized. These must be the Bakers— a more unprepossessing pair I'd not care to meet."

The couple came up to Beth and Mary, wiping their hands on their white aprons—at least they were white once upon a time—though their hands were quite dry.

They performed deep cringing bows and the man said: "Yer ladyships, I be Baker, the caretaker, and I bid ye welcome ter Gryfynskepe. I has me orders ter see as how ye are made all comfortable and such be my intention. Er-ah-we 'ud appreciate it, the missus and me ef, when ye see all is ter yer likin', ye'll favor us wi' a good word in his lordship's ear. He don't know we be very fond of our places and serves the best as is in our power. The late master, blessed be the kind old soul, was allus that pleased with us, and we be sure ef his lordship was to hear a kind word from yer ladyships in our behalf, he'll not be putting us out." After this remarkable speech of welcome, the pair cringed into another salute.

"Thank you, Baker," responded Miss Elizabeth, "but please disabuse yourself that I have anything to say to the marquis. I am here only for the purpose of examining the late Mr. Quarnell's collection of ancient papers. There is such a collection?"

Baker blinked and his wife gasped.

With a hollow laugh, Baker exclaimed: "Oh, aye, there be such. Two rooms full of the nasty things —all dust and spiders—and they be all worthless and only fit to wrap fish with. Sure, a lady'd never think to even touch the old things, what with dirt and great black beetles nestin' in 'em; it's enough to give a decent body the shivers!"

"Ugh! How horrid!" exclaimed Mary.

"Indeed, that is something less than appealing to me; nonetheless, that is why I have come and that is what I propose to do," declared Elizabeth coolly, looking hard at Baker.

"Oh, well of course, yer ladyship—if that be yer pleasure. An' I'd be pleased to help ye any way I can."

"Thank you, but it is not the sort of work that can be shared—unless, of course, you have had experience examining old deeds, writs and what-have-you?"

"Er—no, yer ladyship," said Baker with a baffled look upon his face.

"You, Baker! Get on about your business and do not keep the ladies waiting upon the doorstep!"

commanded Cowles, coming back from seeing that
the horses had been properly cared for. "A thousand pardons, my ladies. If I had known he was such
an oaf, I'd have seen to your care before this."

Baker, nodding his head rapidly more than once,
cried: "Yes, Mr. Cowles; certainly, Mr. Cowles,"
and he and his wife retreated into the house, he
holding the door open while everyone trooped
inside.

Immediately, Cowles began rapping out orders
and, in a very short time, the baggage was being
transported into the recesses of the place while Elizabeth and Mary looked about them in ever-growing
dismay. The exterior of Gryfynskepe had promised
little, and its interior, they discovered, lived up to
that promise and not a bit more.

The place was dim and the air so stale it was
thick; nor was it helped by heavy draperies and
wood paneling and plaster, so dark with age and
reeking of mold that, despite the large size of this
first chamber they were in, the walls seemed to close
in upon them.

Either Cowles must have read their thoughts or
must have, himself, been impressed very much as
they were, for his very next orders were concerned
with lighting lamps and fires.

When all was seen to, he turned to Elizabeth and
Mary.

"For the sake of my Lord Montreat, I offer

apologies, Miss Elizabeth. The Bakers are never up to the standards my lord sets for his retainers. I will see that they give you no trouble. What are your orders, Miss Elizabeth?"

"You are asking *me*?"

"Yes, Miss Elizabeth. I am at your service."

She blinked in puzzlement. "From the manner of your commanding our journey, I was sure I was under yours," she said with a laugh.

He smiled. "I beg your pardon if I gave you that impression, but I took charge in accordance with my lord's instructions to see to your comfort and well-being. Beyond that, you are mistress here."

"Pray tell me, Cowles, it appears to me his lordship places great reliance on you. Surely you are more than footman?"

"Quite, Miss Elizabeth. I see that you are confused because I appeared in that role when I brought your parcels up to your chambers that first day. Actually I am his lordship's man of affairs. I do whatever needs doing as his lordship may direct."

Elizabeth cocked an eye at him. "A man of affairs? Am I to understand you assist his lordship in *all* of his endeavors," she asked archly.

For all his military bearing, Cowles was suddenly very ill at ease.

Elizabeth sought to help him out. "I do not suppose Lord Montreat needs any help at all in certain quarters."

"Oh, Beth, do not tease the poor man!" protested Mary with great impatience. "And do let us go to our rooms. They cannot be any worse than the one we are standing in right now, and I would rest."

Cowles led them up a short, broad staircase to the upper floor. Here the overall squatness of the structure was evidenced by the low ceilings. All the chambers were along the outer walls and surrounded the vaulted upper section of the great room they had been in a moment ago.

Their rooms were ready but not at all fresh-smelling. There was a vertiable miasma of mustiness pervading Gryfynskepe, and one had the feeling it was quite permanent. Airing out the place would probably not not have helped a bit. Nothing short of razing the structure to the ground and starting afresh would remedy it, thought Elizabeth.

Cowles left them and in a little while their maids came to attend them. Having got themselves unpacked and changed into fresh clothing, they laid themselves down to rest for an hour or two. But a series of gigantic thunderclaps brought them upright in their beds, and they stared at each other in fright as the storm, which had been brewing from the moment they arrived, finally unleashed itself and began to roar about the building. Gryfynskepe appeared to welcome the onslaught of the elements and echoed to the wilder notes of the gusting wind's mad threnody. Ghostly currents of air stirred all about in muted imitation of the howling fury without.

As one, both ladies arose and prepared to descend. Their two maids shared their uneasiness and did not remain in these upper chambers any longer than was absolutely necessary.

It was quite dark when they came down. The afternoon was well along, but dusk would still have been some hours off except that the storm had completely blotted out the sun. Passing an embrasure set in the wall near the stairs, they could see out. The heavy, boiling, dark gray sky, split with glimmering cracks of lightning, did nothing to restore their composure. So frequent were the brilliant discharges that they were near blinded, and made the interior seem even darker than before. There was a constant rumble of thunder marked by an occasional earth-shaking peal.

After one such, despite her unease, Elizabeth could not forbear a burst of laughter.

Mary looked at her in surprise.

"Truly, Mary, it is just too, too Gothic. The weather, this building! It is overdoing it, I do declare."

"Well, I, for one, could wish myself somewhere else at this moment. Gryfynskepe and the weather add up to more than I find comfortable."

They found Cowles, lamp in hand, in the corridor leading out of the great room. He smiled when he saw them approach.

"That's a real smasher brewing up outside! We arrived just in time to escape it. I daresay it will blow a deal harder before it lets up and, if I know these parts, it will be morning before it is over."

"What a cheery prospect!" remarked Elizabeth dryly.

"I hope you found your rooms comfortable, my ladies."

Mary retorted: "Well, I hope that my cousin can accomplish her purpose quickly so that we shall not have to stay here any longer than we must!"

Immediately Cowles was all apology, and the ladies had to take pains to assure him that the rooms were satisfactory, but that Gryfynskepe was not a place either of them could be quite at ease in.

Cowles laughed. "Aye, that is easily understood. I fear it has taken on the character of its last occupant, or perhaps it was quite the other way around. The late Mr. Quarnell was, by all accounts, as gloomy as his residence. Well, when the weather clears, it will not be quite so bad. You will be able to go out upon the grounds. There are some delightful views to be had because of its elevation. On a clear day you can see the spires of Bath in the distance."

"Since we cannot, at the moment, is there some small room, not quite so desolate as those we have seen, where we can while away the hours before dinner?" asked Beth.

"I am sorry, Miss Elizabeth, but the kitchen is the best place there is to offer. Fortunately, it is large and does not share the cheerlessness of the rest of the place—but perhaps you would wish to go about the premises? I should be pleased to serve as your guide."

"Oh, that would be nice of you, Mr. Cowles!" declared Mary eagerly.

"I think it would be wiser if we looked into the two fabulous rooms. After all, the sooner started the sooner ended, Mary."

"True enough."

"One moment, please, while I fetch the keys," said Cowles, and he went off after handing the lamp to Mary.

His absence appeared to be a signal for the shadows to grow deeper and infinitely more menacing. The two girls, in unspoken accord, joined their hands together for greater comfort.

It was almost a quarter of an hour later that Cowles returned, carrying a great bunch of enormous brass keys threaded upon a thick iron ring.

At the sight of them, Beth remarked: "They would be quite appropriate for a dungeon."

Cowles chuckled. "I daresay you are right. The very name of the place bespeaks such an origin, and its subsequent owners did little in the way of disguising it."

"Yes, the sculptures upon the outer walls look more like horrid bats than griffins!" declared Mary.

As Cowles conducted them along the corridor and then turned down a narrower one, he said: "There is something strange about that man, Baker. I am not sure what he is about, but, whatever it is, I am sure I do not like it."

"He is certainly a most unattractive specimen, but what is it that you have discovered?" asked Beth.

"When I requested the keys of him, the idiot made a great show of going through his pockets, as though anyone could carry such a load as these"— he held up the keys and rattled them noisily—"in one's pocket. Then he tried to tell me that he must have misplaced them. Naturally, I would not stand still for his nonsense, and he finally fetched them. He is not very bright, but that little episode struck me as quite imbecilic."

"Perhaps you give him too much credit," suggested Elizabeth.

"Perhaps. Ah, here we are! This is the first room."

He brought the keys up into the light of the lamp in Mary's hand. He paused, looking at them uncertainly.

"God rot the fool! Which of them is it? There are over a dozen here, I'll swear, and there is not a clue as to which is which! Well, by your leave, ladies, I'll seek the fellow out—"

"No! No!" protested Elizabeth and Mary together. "Do not leave us!"

Elizabeth offered: "One of them has got to work if we are patient, I am sure."

Cowles grinned. "Very well, I shall try them one at a time," and he proceeded to do so. He went through the ring without success the first time and proceeded to try them all once again.

When he had done, he was looking very puzzled. He turned to the girls. "You saw? I tried each and every one—twice to be sure—but not a one of them will turn in the lock. Where is that clod, Baker?" he demanded and went stalking off, very angry.

The girls were not about to be left behind, and they hurried after him. He led them to the kitchen.

"Where is Baker?" he demanded of the cook.

She informed him with a puzzled air that the Bakers had gone out upon an errand that he, himself, had set them.

"I did no such thing!" he exclaimed, his choler mounting. "I begin to suspect he is up to no good and fears discovery. Come! We shall see what has been going on!" he declared, picking up the massive kitchen poker as he strode from the room.

As they proceeded back along the corridor, Elizabeth remarked: "I knew the setting was too perfect!

It just begs for arcane intrigue. Truly, we could have done well enough without another mystery. The place is awful enough in itself. To have some penny-dreadful hugger-mugger into the bargain is really going beyond the bounds of good taste."

Arriving at the door to the room, Cowles went quickly to work, applying the poker to the door as a pry bar. It took some effort, for the door was as massive as all the other appointments of Gryfynskepe, but he finally succeeded, and the door swung open with a hair-raising screech.

He took the lamp from Mary and, holding it high over his head, stepped into the room. Just then the thunder cracked so loudly, everyone jumped, even Cowles.

"Hah!" he exclaimed. "The devil is out tonight!" Then he laughed as he saw the ashen faces of the girls glimmering in the light of the lamp. "Oh, come now, Miss Elizabeth! Miss Mary! It is just a saying! There is nought to be afraid of."

"I am quite sure you are right, Cowles. At least my reason says it is so. If only I could convince my craven heart," replied Elizabeth with an attempt at levity. "Will you look at all those stacks and stacks of manuscripts!"

As far as the lamplight could reach, corded bundles of aged documents—here and there, the glint of a seal and the hint of a bit of ribbon catching the eye—reached as high as a man's head. Some few bundles, broken and scattered, lay just beyond the doorway, their twine undone.

"So that's his game, is it?" exclaimed Cowles, bending over them. "He has been going through them, for they were not disturbed when my lord and I inspected these rooms last. Come, let us move to the next room and see how it has fared."

Cowles quickly forced the door of the second repository, and the sight that greeted them plainly indicated the chamber had been thoroughly ransacked. There was no order to it at all. Sheets were piled helter-skelter all about, all of them obviously examined and discarded. The room had been quite thoroughly gone over.

"Well, Baker has got the sack—although I'll hazard a guess he knows it already and has skipped out with his spouse. My lord is not going to like this at all."

"I cannot say I am *un*happy about it. From the appearance of the two rooms, it is evident that whatever it is we are looking for has not been found. Since one room is plenty to have to study, anyone who works to reduce the length of my stay at Gryfynskepe has my undying gratitude," declared Elizabeth.

"But, Miss Elizabeth, what could Baker have known about anything? Surely he has not the expertise to judge the value of these parchments. I *know* he cannot read, so he could not distinguish between a draper's receipt and the Magna Carta, itself!"

"I do not doubt what you say is true, and it is a puzzle why Baker should have made the attempt. Did my Lord Montreat mention the business of the strange offer he received for Gryfynskepe? Since you claim to be his man of affairs, I assume you know to what I refer."

"Aye. You may rest assured my lord had not a word of conversation with Baker when he was here. It was left with me to deal with him, and I certainly would never discuss my master's business with the likes of him—or almost anyone else."

Elizabeth smiled. "I see you have no such reservation regarding us."

"It pleases me to say, Miss Elizabeth and Miss Mary, my instructions were quite specific on that score. I am to treat with you as though you were —er-members of the family."

"Well, Mary, what do you think of that?" asked Elizabeth chuckling. "How does it feel to be regarded as a Montreat?"

"I beg your pardon, my lady, but the name is Quarnell."

"Of course. How silly of me not to have used it. But this is not the first time you have addressed me as 'my lady,' Cowles—or, perhaps, it would be in better taste to address you as Mr. Cowles?"

"If it please you, Miss Elizabeth," he responded,

with a bow. It was not particularly courtly, being too stiff, but it was one of respect.

"You have not answered me, Mr. Cowles."

"I beg you pardon, my—Miss Elizabeth. I am sure it is only a slip of the tongue. I shall guard myself on that score if it annoys you."

Elizabeth laughed lightly. "No, it does not annoy me, but I daresay it can prove embarrassing were you to do so in the hearing of others. *I* have no pretensions to nobility."

"Exactly so, Miss Elizabeth." And although his face wore its usual sober expression, to Elizabeth it seemed as though his eyes were dancing.

"To get back to the puzzle of Baker then, one is forced to conclude that, in the time between your last visit and now, he has come into possession of knowledge that appears to confirm my lord's suspicions."

Cowles began to knit his brows. "Do you say he knew exactly what he was looking for?"

"Let us suppose there was some description of treasure, or even something more subtle, afloat in this mess, would you trust Baker to recognize it? And having found it, would you trust him to share it with you?"

"No, by damn!—A thousand pardons!—But I think you have hit upon it. There has got to be another party involved and, more likely than not, whoever he is, he did the searching himself. You are quick, Miss Elizabeth. My compliments to you."

"Thank you, Mr. Cowles. You are too kind. It is only that I was trying so desperately hard to find an excuse not to have to go through this room as well as the other."

"You see, Mr. Cowles, where the cleverness in our family reposes," remarked Mary. "*I* never would have suspected so much and would have resigned myself to the full task."

"Then I do not feel so lacking," said Mr. Cowles, "for I am sure I should have done the same as you." There was more than kindliness in his tone.

The dim, sparse light hid Mary's blush of pleasure, but not Elizabeth's warm smile.

"Dinner should be waiting, I think. Whilst you ladies partake, I shall run down to Combe Hay and make inquiries as to Baker's whereabouts. I hardly expect he'll return here willingly. I hope to get from him the information he appears to have. It must lighten your task considerably if you know exactly what it is you are searching for."

"It would be of considerable help, Mr. Cowles, but I pray you will not be long at it. I am sure I speak for my cousin as well as myself when I say we feel more secure for your presence."

"Thank you, my lady. I will not be long."

ॐ

"How do you like the food?" asked Elizabeth as they sat alone at table in the small dining room. Strange to say, it was situated just off the kitchen and was the only bit of rational design about the place. It did not lessen their sense of security to hear the banging of pots and pans beyond the walls, indicating the presence of friendly beings close at hand.

"It is most excellent," responded Mary.

Nor had it hurt the viands that they could be served up so conveniently. Cook was at no pains to keep them hot while they were carried the lengths of chilly corridors as was the practice in so many of the larger homes of the day.

"My lord's taste in servants is extremely nice, and we must be grateful he did not stint to see to our comfort," remarked Elizabeth.

"Well, we need not be *too* grateful!"

Elizabeth laughed. "But, Mary, we must be reasonable. Look about you! Gryfynskepe is a most unlikely place to foster romance, illicit or otherwise. No, I am become quite convinced that the marquis had only business in mind, sending us out here, and that is how I shall deal with him."

"You are forgetting how deeply in debt you are to him. If it is just business, how can you ever begin to repay him? I will admit that my Lord Rakehell and Gryfynskepe are an odd combination, to say the least, but I do not see that it changes *your* prospects all that much."

"I-I could wish you would not refer to him by that disgusting title, Mary."

"I must and I shall, my love. I do not like to hear it any better than you do, but you must be kept on your guard against the man. I do not see that anything has changed so that you can begin to place your trust in him."

Elizabeth sighed. "Perhaps it is his not being with us. Absence, perhaps, is making him appear-er-well, it would be nice if he was at table with us. He-he has a way of lightening the air, don't you think?"

Mary looked askance at her cousin. "I suppose any company would be of help in this cavern. I-I wonder whether Mr. Cowles will be dining with us. I see that no cover was set for him, and I, for one, did not think it was all that necessary for him to seek out that horrid Baker person in all this storm and darkness."

Elizabeth reached across and grasped Mary's hand.

"I daresay, my dear, if I insisted, he would dine with us in the future. Do you wish it?"

Mary jerked her hand free of her cousin's. "I am sure it does not matter to me! If you agree that a gentleman's company at table is desirable—and I am sure he is a gentleman despite the menial tasks the marquis sets him—I'll not object."

"Mary, it is I, your beloved cousin Elizabeth. Please do not put on such airs with me, but speak plainly. Have I ever done other with you?"

Mary smiled shamefacedly. "I should love to have Mr. Cowles at table, dearest cousin."

Even as they regarded each other with warm affection and understanding, they heard a door slam shut and, shortly, Mr. Cowles made his appearance. He was dripping wet and his face looked stern.

"Ladies, I am sorry to have to intrude upon you—"

"You are wet, Mr. Cowles!" cried Mary. "Please see to yourself before you catch your death! But, first, may I offer you some brandy to warm you? It is the one thing besides parchment Uncle Ethelbert had in great store."

"Thank you, Miss Mary. This is most kind of you. But before I change to dry things, I have some rather frightful news to impart."

"Pray be seated, Mr. Cowles," said Elizabeth.

"But I am drenched—"

"If Uncle Ethelbert will not object, I shall not. Please, Mr. Cowles."

"With pleasure, Miss Elizabeth."

He seated himself and accepted a glass of spirits from Mary. It was filled to the brim, but he downed it in two or three great draughts, after which he blew out his cheeks with a whoosh! Then he laughed.

"Heaven help the man you marry, Miss Mary! Your generosity with a glass of cheer must certainly put him under the table and keep him there!"

"Oh dear! I did not know. Was it too much?"

"Not this once, for I certainly needed a skinful! It is all up with Baker!"

"Great God, man! Did you kill him?" exclaimed Elizabeth.

"Indeed not, nor had I any such intention. It was a greater hand than mine that did the deed—the greatest! Both he and his wife are dead of a lightning bolt. They had not got fifty paces from the house before they were struck. It was a sight I'll not describe, nor do I care if I never see the like again."

"How-how could you be sure it was the lightning?" asked Elizabeth.

"The least unpleasant detail I dare impart to you is the condition of the keys. He had been carrying them in his hand when he was struck down. It must have been a fearful blow, for his hand had all the appearance of being encased in a brazen glove. Just that brassy horror is all that is left of the missing keys."

"Oh, the poor man! How awful for him and his wife!"

"Oh, I hardly think they could have had any idea of what struck them. They must have been killed on the instant. Well, that puts an end to any information from him. Although I'd not wish such an end to him or to any man, yet I am relieved that he is out of the house. I do hope my lord does not delay getting down here. I am not at all pleased with these developments."

"Wh-where are they now?"

"I left them where they rest. There is nought I can do for them in this weather, and *they* cannot mind it. I'll see to them first thing in the morning."

"I think you had better get into some dry things now, Mr. Cowles," suggested Mary anxiously.

"Thank you for your concern, Miss Mary, but do not worry yourself over it. I have served in wet clothes for weeks on end under the tropical monsoons of India. But if it will ease your mind, I'll see to it."

"After you have changed, I'll make you a hot toddy—if-if you like."

"Indeed I should and very much. I'll change that much faster, and thank you, dear lady."

ॐ

The storm was well past, the next morning, leaving a brightly polished sun to lighten the air and find its way through the narrow casements to dispel some part of the murkiness of the old building.

The slumbers of Elizabeth and Mary were not

disturbed until the sun was well up, and it came about from noise upon the grounds without. Mr. Cowles had been to Combe Hay and returned with the justice of the peace and a group of locals to assist him in the examination and removal of the bodies.

It was a most sobering fashion in which to be roused from slumber, and the girls had little to say as they prepared to go down for breakfast.

At the table, Mary gave the appearance of being vexed about something.

Elizabeth inquired: "Do you wish us to leave, cousin?"

Mary looked up from her dish and quickly shook her head.

Elizabeth frowned in perplexity. "Then whatever is troubling you? I admit the fate of the Bakers sometimes makes one wonder whose turn it will be next, but if it is God's will—No! That is too unctuous of me! I should have said—"

"Oh, Beth, it is not that! I understand it and need no comforting. I am just amazed that we are dining alone again."

"Cowles? Well, he is detained by the business outside."

"There are still only two covers," Mary stated flatly.

"I pray you, Mary, do not look at me as though I were guilty of some horrendous crime. I have not had a chance to invite him to dine with us. If you will wipe away that scowl, I shall certainly do so the very next time I see him—or would you have me rush right out there and implore him to come to table on the instant?"

"Now you are being silly, Beth!" responded Mary very primly. "An informal invitation at your convenience will do very nicely."

"I have a much better idea. Why do you not invite him yourself?"

Mary looked fearful. "Oh, I could not! I could never be so fast!"

"Fast? I see! It is perfectly all right if I am fast?"

"No, Beth! Oh dear, I did not mean—You-you have no difficulty speaking to him."

Elizabeth laughed. "All you have to do is to believe that he is in dire need of our company, and you will find it quite easy to speak with him."

"I do not understand what you mean."

"You had no difficulty speaking to him, last night, when you thought he was in great need of changing into dry things, and your offer of the hot toddy was positively daring!"

"Elizabeth!" cried Mary, blushing furiously.

"There, there, do not upset yourself. I'll see to it. For now, I am going to leave you and begin my task with the parchments. I am sure it is time since it is work that has already been more than paid for. What do you plan to do?"

"If you do not mind, I should like to come along with you. I am sure I can be of assistance."

"I have not the least objection, and I should be glad for your company."

❦

Elizabeth's mother had been an intelligent woman, but of a consumptive cast of health. As she approached her middle years—which she never achieved—she had become bedridden and, seeming to appreciate the inevitability of having to leave her beloved husband and child before long, she encouraged her daughter to interest herself in Mr. Brown's well-being and in his vocation. The long hours of loneliness that she thus had to endure during each day were more than made up to her by Elizabeth's burgeoning interest in the shop and in its customers. The child would come home with her father and regale her with all that went on in the shop, and it became an entertainment for her as well as an opportunity to advise, suggest and recommend to Elizabeth upon the ways of the world as they were exhibited in the milieu of the little establishment.

When at last her Maker summoned her and she departed, her passing made no appreciable stir in the arrangement of the Brown menage, but the impress upon the hearts and minds of her husband and daughter was indelible, and their mutual sorrow worked to make the bond between them even stronger.

Mary Vernon, a distant cousin with an income so tiny as to make it hardly worthy of the term "independence," was at the time engaged as a governess upon an estate in Norfolk. She had never been to London in her life and, being somewhat plain of feature, had little prospect of finding a spouse amongst the gentry of her acquaintance. They were all of them too high and wealthy to look to a governess for wife, and her breeding and station would not permit her to entertain the prospect of a husband from amongst the yeomanry. When she received an invitation from her only surviving male relative to join his establishment in Bloomsbury, she accepted with alacrity, matrimony being not the last thing in her mind.

But Mr. Brown, who was more up to the knocker with his bookish ways might lead one to think, had something else in mind. His Elizabeth was of an age when the continuing counsel of a mature female was most necessary, and it was a task quite beyond his powers. Although Mary Vernon was not so very much older than Elizabeth, yet she was old enough to be accounted a woman, whereas his daughter still had some years to go before she herself had reached that state.

In the end, Mary came to satisfy a desire—in which she was disappointed—but remained to become a firmly established member of the Brown household. Mr. Brown was a warm and cordial gentleman, and Elizabeth, she discovered, was a charming child if somewhat intense. In a very little time there developed within her an affection for Elizabeth that was at once something maternal, something sisterly and something that was truly amicable in a larger sense than either. There was a complete lack of rivalry between them and, despite the disparity in years, there existed a great ease of mutual understanding.

By the time Mr. Brown departed to join his late wife, the two girls had grown accustomed to living together in a most contented fashion. There was no strict separation of duties between them, but Elizabeth's bent was more for the shop and Mary's for homemaking and so, helping each other out, they had managed up to the moment to get along in reasonable comfort, but barely.

As they began the examination of the documents, it was understood that anything Mary discovered that was not obviously worthless, she would set aside for Elizabeth's detailed appraisal.

Their first efforts were brought to an end abruptly when one of the great stacks, suddenly overbalanced, came toppling down with a resounding thump, raising such billows of dust as to make breathing impossible. All achoke and coughing until tears filled their eyes, they were forced to withdraw so as to permit things to settle and the air to clear.

"Oh dear!" exclaimed Elizabeth wiping her eyes. "Wasn't that awful? Look at our clothes! We are all over dust!" She began to giggle. "At this rate we shall be a year at it! The dust is so thick in there and the light so poor and the writing so faint, I daresay we shall be all headachy and stifled for ever so long!"

Mary smiled. "It is not a good beginning for Lord Montreat, that is sure! We have been at it three hours, and I do not think I have gotten through more than a few dozen of the dusty rags. How many have you done?"

"Not as many, I fear. They are extremely fascinating. I cannot help speculating about the inscribers and the recipients, for many of them are quite old and they tell a story—many stories, I think."

"You have found something of value? I have not. They are mainly bills of trade and leases with, here and there, a note of some more personal nature, as near as I have been able to decipher."

Elizabeth shook her head. "Oh, Mary, how can you dismiss them so lightly? They have so much to tell us. I could spend hours on each one, imagining why they were written and what the people who were concerned with them were like—their stations in life, their connections, their households. . . ."

"It is just as well that I do not have your predilection or we shall never finish."

They went up to their chambers where they began to change into fresh garments.

"I shall ask my lord, after we have done, if I may have them. I cannot bear to think of them being carted off by some irreverent rag dealer."

"Beth, are you quite mad? Where in the world should we keep them? Never in our chambers in Bloomsbury, and the shop is quite filled up as it is."

"Of course I do not say I wish to keep all! There is much that can be discarded, I am sure, but there are certain of them that tell so much of a forgotten time. I must have spent all of a quarter of an hour upon a draft from a merchant; it must have been drawn up for his wife—or perhaps his mistress— It was made out to one Mrs. Smithers, seamstress, and described in detail a gown close on a hundred years ago. I did not know what half the terms meant. And then there are household accounts of even greater age. It would be most interesting to compare them with accounts in this our day, to see how the day-to-day living has changed."

"It is interesting," agreed Mary, "but not so much so that I would care to spend the rest of my life at it, here in Gryfynskepe."

"No, you are quite right. I shall have to make a greater effort to get through them. It is too bad about the Bakers—I mean, how much trouble could be spared us if we had an idea of the sort of thing we are looking for. Perhaps, when my lord arrives, he will have something to suggest—now that his suspicions have had such drastic confirmation."

"Well, I think we should ask Mr. Cowles to arrange it so that the stacks are made more secure. I should hate to have a repetition of this morning's disaster, especially when either of us could be the victim of the odious avalanche instead of merely spectators."

୫ଛ

Mr. Cowles was able to shore up the stacks with some odd pieces of lumber, and they were enabled to resume their studies in safety. They worked hours on end, halting their labors when their eyes began to smart, or when the slight movements they made in transferring the documents about finally stirred up so much dust into the air that breathing became uncomfortable. The windows at the far end of the room were of no help as they were thoroughly blocked up by the masses of parchment. To have reached them would have required half-emptying the room and hauling the remainder away from the narrow openings. No one thought it to be worth the effort, especially as the size of the two casements did not promise much in the way of ventilation.

It was just as well for, when conditions became unbearable, they took advantage of the interruptions to take leisurely walks about the place. The weather had turned delightful, and they could see miles across the low hills and vales from their vantage on Gryfynskepe's rise. Here and there, a church spire thrust its spike up from a mass of greenery that obscured the village surrounding its base. It was all rather restful and pretty.

When the weekend arrived, an air of expectancy gripped the girls. My Lord Montreat had promised to come then, and, for different reasons, each young lady had very much in mind his impending visit.

When Saturday was come to a close and my lord had not put in an appearance, nor had any word been received concerning his arrival, Mr. Cowles looked disturbed and the girls disappointed. Elizabeth was puzzled that, as hard as she might try, she could not resurrect in any great detail the aspect of his countenance. It surprised her greatly. She had only the strong impression of his charm and of his masculinity, but she could not for her life's sake recall more than a mere impression of his flashing dark eyes or his brilliant smile. It was a matter of the greatest importance that she see him again, to refresh her memory of him in the greatest detail.

Mary, on the other hand, had some hope that his

lordship would either have lost his patience with their lack of progress or be able to supply some clue that would facilitate the work. In either case, it would provide excuse to shorten their stay at Gryfynskepe and—something she devoutly wished —bring to an end his lordship's unfortunate interest in Elizabeth.

Sunday was no better and on Monday, Elizabeth and Mary were quite subdued as they began to take up the work once more.

"What do you think?" asked Mary as she perused an ancient lease for a cottage in Suffolk.

"About what?" asked Elizabeth, staring fixedly at the document she held, complete with seal and faded bit of ribbon.

"Beth, I can see that your mind is not on the parchments. It is on something else."

Elizabeth smiled slightly. "I do not wonder that he is delayed, only that he has not seen fit to apprise us," she remarked without preface.

Mary shrugged. "I say the wonder of it is that he has gone to such expense with us—with you. It is *not* surprising that his interest has waned. I do not think my Lord Montreat has any need to be persistent in his endeavors. He can assuage his appetite in another direction for the mere turning about."

"I suppose it is as you say, but I should like to know for sure."

When they assembled in the dining room, Mr.

Cowles was not present and Mary began to look blue.

"Cousin, must you wear your heart on your sleeve so?" asked Elizabeth. "It is most unseemly. Do not look at me as though it were my fault still!"

"Then why does he not dine with us?" demanded Mary.

"My dear, I assure you that I invited him to join us whenever he likes, but I did not command him to do so. If he elects not to, that is his business, and you are well advised to understand what his absence means. Truly, Mary, although I do not find Mr. Cowles in any way exceptionable, still it is not as though he were some great prize. I am sure he is past his fortieth year and must be quite accustomed to life without a fair partner—or is he married?"

"No, he is not and-and he has been so-so kind to me, I am sure his interest is more than a casual one."

"I am not saying it is not but, to what extent, I caution you to reserve your judgment. If you go on in this way, you are bound to break your heart."

"It is my heart and I shall do as I like!" retorted Mary, very petulantly.

Elizabeth smiled understandingly. "I suppose I should be the last to challenge anyone on that score, for I am in no better case."

At that moment, Mr. Cowles entered. From his dress it was obvious he had been out riding.

"My apologies, ladies, for being late, but I

thought it wise to go down to Combe Hay and see if any letters had come."

Mary's face took on a sparkle, and she shot a superior glance at Elizabeth who was saying: "How very thoughtful of you, Mr. Cowles. Will you not join us?"

"I should be most happy to do so, Miss Elizabeth, but as you see I am dusty and—"

"I assure you that is not the least objectionable to me. But perhaps Mary. . . ?" and she raised a questioning eyebrow at her cousin.

Mary immediately responded with a most cordial invitation, one that could not have been easily refused without giving offense.

Mr. Cowles thanked them and took his seat. He reached into his pocket and withdrew a sealed letter which he handed to Elizabeth.

It was from the marquis and was franked by the Duke of Verndon.

She inquired of Mr. Cowles: 'Who is the Duke of Verndon?"

"He is sire to the marquis."

"Oh, then Lord Montreat is not a peer in his own right?"

"No, he is heir to the duke."

Elizabeth felt a wave of disappointment wash over her. If a marquis was higher than anyone she might ever dream of wedding, how much more beyond her expectations must be the rank of duchess for her?

She broke the wafer and quickly perused the contents. Whatever she might have expected, the letter came nowhere near. It was coldly formal and quite terse. She was informed that his lordship was unavoidably detained, and he instructed her to proceed with her studies. She was to look to Cowles for anything she might require. It closed with:—I remain your most affectionate servant—Tony— and she had to be satisfied that that last signaled some warmth of feeling for her. But it was not much, and it gave her to wonder if his ardor was not cooling. Without a word of comment, she handed it first to Mary and then to Cowles.

Neither had anything to say, but both looked uneasy. Elizabeth felt very discontented and wished to pursue the matter.

"I do not suppose it is unusual for his lordship to be distracted from his engagements?" she asked of Cowles.

He appeared startled but answered, nevertheless: "He is his own master, Miss Elizabeth."

"I daresay and, like the proverbial sailor, is never far from the solace of feminine companionship, except that ports and storms are no inconveniences to him."

"If by that you imply that he is detained by some

inamorata, I can hardly agree. He is at Oaklands, you know."

"Oaklands? Where is that, may I ask?"

"It is the Quarnell family seat in Kent."

"Knowing his lordship as I do, I do not see that Oaklands or any place else would act to dampen my Lord Montreat's-er-activities, if you know what I mean."

Cowles, with a half-smile, responded: "Well, you are out there. At Oaklands, my lord is ever on his best behavior. The duke and the duchess are in residence there."

"What have they to say to anything my lord Montreat may wish to do? He is completely impervious to the opinion of others. I am sure he did not get that way for any control his parents might have had over him."

"I will not venture to say that their Graces are, or are not, concerned over my lord's manner of living in London, but this I will say: Where my Lady Elvira is concerned, not the marquis, not the duke himself will do aught to embarrass her. In fact I do not know *anyone* who can stand against her for very long."

"Indeed Her Grace must be a most formidable female!" exclaimed Mary.

Cowles laughed good-naturedly. "In a manner of speaking, I suppose she is, though I am sure that no one ever thinks of her in that way. You will meet her some day, Miss Mary, and judge her for yourself."

"I? Meet the Duchess of Verndon? What can you be thinking, Mr. Cowles?"

"I am thinking that if I have anything to say to it, you shall most certainly be presented to my Lady Elvira, one day," he declared, conferring a meaningful look upon Mary.

Elizabeth was too puzzled over his remark to have observed his expression. She asked: "Do you say Her Grace would receive an-er-ah-acquaintance of *yours*, Mr. Cowles? I find that condescending in her beyond what is believable."

"Miss Elizabeth, my place with the Quarnells is, I am honored to say, one of high trust and confidence. I look upon my duty as being anything concerned with keeping Lord Montreat from harm. I have not been with the Quarnells so long as to claim the prerogatives of an old family retainer, but I am more of a companion to his lordship than a servant —but I should prefer not to bore you on this matter longer."

"I assure you, Mr. Cowles, I am not bored. In fact, I am greatly puzzled. It would seem to me that your place would be at Oaklands by his lordship's side than here at Gryfynskepe playing at bearleader to two inconsequential females."

"My dear Miss Elizabeth, I fear I have already said more than is fitting. I shall add only that I do not question my lord's instructions and, further, that this duty is in no way onerous to me."

"I beg your pardon. I had not meant to pry. Well, Mary, if we are done with our lunch, I suggest we recommence with the business of earning our fee, don't you think?"

*

The week that followed was a quiet one and, although the two cousins spent all their time at the stacks of yellowing sheets, not all that much was accomplished. They had little to say to each other as they perused one document after another. They each appeared to be closeted with their own thoughts, and communication between them became a most absentminded affair.

Late Friday afternoon, her eyes burning in her head like live coals and her back weary to the point of aching from the uncomfortable business of hunching over the parchments, Elizabeth finally put the work from her and arose wearily.

"I have had enough!" she declared.

"And I, too!" exclaimed Mary, following suit.

"There is nothing in any of this of great value! I am prepared to call a halt and go back to London."

"Oh no! It is much too soon!" protested Mary.

"We have but barely begun! Why we have yet to complete the first stack! And what of your great debt to his lordship?"

"Let him worry about it! I shan't!"

"But, Elizabeth, bethink you! He could have us thrown into the Marshalsea for debt, and we could never get out! We should lose our shop, everything!"

"How would that serve him? He would not be a farthing the richer for it."

"Well, I still say it is much too soon!"

"What, do you enjoy this muddling about in old papers and the dust of ages?"

"No, of course I do not, but it has all been paid for."

Elizabeth eyed her cousin speculatively. "Can there be something more here? You have been so very quiet this past week, I wonder."

Mary blushed. "It is true I have been given to thinking."

"Of Mr. Cowles, no doubt."

"Well, yes—in a way—it was what he said. I-I am not sure that I understood his meaning."

"What did he say?"

"You recall it was Monday. We were at lunch and he said—he said if he had anything to do with it, I should meet Her Grace. Do not you think it was a strange thing for him to say?"

"Ye-es, it was. But if *you* find it so strange, why have you not asked him what he meant by it?"

"Oh dear, I could never. What would he think of me? I could never be so forward."

"Well, I can. Shall I ask him?" Elizabeth was smiling slightly.

"Beth, I pray you let it lay. I am sure if Mr. Cowles m-meant anything at all by it, he will explain himself in due time."

"And so, my sweet, we must continue our dusty labors until he gets around to it, I take it."

Mary looked at her cousin, and there was a plea in her eyes. In a small voice she said: "If you do not mind."

"Well, I have had enough of this business to do *me* for a day or two. I propose that we visit Bath tomorrow and see the sights."

"Oh, I should love that!" exclaimed Mary, beaming with pleasure.

"Would you be brave enough to request of Mr. Cowles that he escort us? It will not hurt to have a guide, nor the presence of a gentleman, if all that I hear of Bath is to be believed."

"I-I should like that very much, Beth. But could it not be you who asks him?"

"No, it could not! If he refuses or accepts *my* invitation, it can mean nothing of any consequence. But it will speak volumes how he responds to an invitation from you!"

"But what if he should refuse me? I should die of mortification!"

"You are made of sterner stuff than that, Mary. Furthermore, it is no great thing. If Mr. Cowles refuses you, why we shall call this business quits and return to London. I am sure you will not wish to prolong your stay here after that."

"Very well, I shall ask him," said Mary very reluctantly.

❧

Elizabeth was quite bored as she sat by herself between two empty chairs. The Assembly Room was quite full this evening, and everyone seemed to know everyone else so that she felt quite left out of things—a perfect stranger. Mr. Cowles and Mary had left her to join in the dancing and, for the moment, she was very much unoccupied.

They had spent the afternoon with Mr. Cowles showing them about Bath, and, while it all was of some interest to Elizabeth, she could not help comparing this minuscule resort town to the great metropolis in which she had resided all her life. Bath was undoubtedly a nice place to visit, but it must have been a deadly place to come to if one had no friends here. Mr. Cowles and Mary seemed quite content to go about and pass all sorts of meaningless remarks about what they saw, and understanding what was between those two, it only made her feel more lonely. For once in her life, Mary appeared to have no thought for her cousin.

Of course, if my Lord Montreat had been *there* with her as he had promised, she was quite sure the visit to Bath would have been a deal more to her taste. But the marquis, for the second weekend in a row, had not put in an appearance. She was very disappointed and did not hesitate to blame all her displeasure upon Tony!

She was stifling a yawn when a gentleman approached and came to stand before her.

"Miss Brown, I believe?" he asked, making a small bow.

She regarded him with some puzzlement. There was something vaguely familiar about his face, but she was sure that she did not know him. All the dashing young gentlemen in her acquaintanceship could be numbered on one finger of one hand.

"Ah, I see you do not recall me. I had the pleasure of seeing you at Claridge's in Tony Quarnell's company. I am George Richards, his very good friend."

She smiled in greeting. "Indeed, I thought you looked familiar, my lord. It is my lord, is it not?"

He laughed. "Yes, but I should prefer you to call me 'George.' After all, it is good enough for Tony.

By the way, is he about? He disappeared from London and no one seems to know where he went off to. Seeing you here, I assume that he is in Bath."

"No, he is not. He is gone to Oaklands for a time."

Lord George looked puzzled. "How comes it that you did not go with him?"

"I, my lord? Whatever for?"

"Well, I only thought that—he did bring you to Claridge's and you are not his usual sort—er, that is—"

Elizabeth burst into delighted laughter. "No, I am not! But what has that to do with—"

"I say, George, old man! So nice to run into you," exclaimed a dapper gentleman, dressed up to the nines, coming up to them, his hand outstretched.

Lord George nodded his head and shook the fellow's hand with less than marked enthusiasm. "Hallo, Harry! What are you doing in Bath? Have the cards been going against you at Watier's?"

"Not a bit! I came down for a bit of business in the neighborhood—but, I say, how about an introduction to this lovely lady?"

"Of course. Miss Brown, may I present Sir Harry Armbruster, a most engaging rascal. Harry, this is Miss Elizabeth Brown, a friend of Montreat's."

"Ah, I am delighted—in truth! I have had my eye upon you all evening, hoping to meet you. I was overjoyed when I saw that you had acquaintance with my very old friend, Lord George."

"I am flattered, Sir Harry."

"I understand you are staying out at Gryfyns-kepe. It is a shame about the Bakers."

"Oh, you know the place?"

"Quite well. I was a guest of Mr. Quarnell more than once while he lived. I say, Miss Brown, would you think it too forward of me if I joined you?"

"Not at all, Sir Harry. I am here with my cousin, Mary Vernon, and a Mr. Cowles. They'd not mind if you sat down, I am sure, as they can hardly have a use for the chairs while they are at dancing."

"Thank you," he said, sitting down, leaving Lord George still standing and looking a bit foolish. My lord had no chance to recover, for with the greatest cheek, Sir Harry remarked: "I say, George, as long as you have nothing to do, be a good fellow and fetch us a round of refreshment. I'll trust you to return with something cooling for us all."

A little line formed on Lord George's brow. "Of course. But Miss Brown, I shall demand the next dance in payment."

"It will be my pleasure, my lord," said Elizabeth with a warm smile.

He went off.

"Oh, I say!" exclaimed Sir Harry in aggrieved tones. "That was cool of him!"

"I thought he came out of it rather well."

"He *saw* that we were engaged."

"We were only conversing. Don't you think it

was rather highhanded of you to send him off the way you did?"

Sir Harry reared back somewhat and stared at Elizabeth with a new interest. "You are a different sort of female, Miss Brown. You do not mince words."

She stared back at him coolly for a moment. "How am I to take that, sir? The import is less than flattering, but the tone is something else again."

He flashed beautiful teeth in a scintillating smile. "You are a most unusual female, indeed!"

Elizabeth chuckled. "There you go again! I do not know how to take you, Sir Harry."

"If I say that you have aroused my interest, my dear, and added charm to this otherwise dull gathering, I think you can take it as most complimentary to yourself, and so it is intended."

"Why, thank you, sir."

"And before I lose a further opportunity, may I have the next dance after?"

"Of course. Are you, too, acquainted with my Lord Montreat?"

"Only by reputation, Miss Brown."

Elizabeth burst into laughter. "Oh dear, what shades of meaning one can take from that so inoffensive-sounding remark."

"Now, indeed, you embarrass me. I know not how to proceed as you are, so I have been given to understand, a friend to his lordship?" His eyebrows went up as though to emphasize the delicate nature of his inquiry.

"Have no fear. I am only a friend to the marquis, if that. In fact, I am sure I am not so much. I am engaged upon a commission for him."

"At Gryfynskepe?"

"Yes."

"I cannot for the life of me imagine what there is for you to do at that dreadful place. Are you studying to redecorate it? If so, you have my deepest sympathy. I do not see how it can be improved short of burning it to the ground and starting all over again."

"I quite agree. No, it is nothing so difficult as all that. I am an antiquarian of sorts. Oh dear, perhaps that is being boastful. I have some experience in old documents and that sort of thing, and Lord Montreat prevailed upon me to examine Mr. Quarnell's collection which, of course, my lord has inherited."

"Do not tell me that Montreat is concerned for anything of value in that pile of refuse! I am surprised he should waste your time in such a fruitless pursuit, especially when any man with half a mind could easily find more pleasurable occupations for your charm and appearance."

Elizabeth doubted the sincerity of his compliments. She had no illusions about her appearance and found his flattery overdone. She ignored it. "You are familiar with the Quarnell collection?"

she asked since this was of more immediate interest to her.

"Old Ethelbert was very proud of it. He made a point of showing me two rooms filled to overflowing with manuscripts of all sorts and descriptions. The more impressive the seal, the longer the ribbons, the prouder he was, I am sure. I should venture to think, Miss Brown, that you are not so taken in by such notions."

"No, of course I am not. There is a fair amount of material there of interest to the historian, I daresay, but until I have finished my examination, I truly cannot say more."

"Then it is not some particular item you are searching for, I take it."

It was a very offhand comment. He even looked about the dance floor as he said it, but it gave Elizabeth pause. She was now very alert to every nuance in his tone.

She said: "You will forgive me, Sir Harry, but it is not for me to disclose anything about the business. It is possible that I have revealed more than my principal would have liked, already."

He turned to her in all apology. "My dear Miss Brown, I beg you not to think I was prying. Of course, I understand the confidential nature of your commission and would not dream of asking you to breach it. It was only idle curiosity on my part."

The dance having ended, Lord George made his

appearance with a filled glass in each hand. He gave one to Elizabeth and proceeded to take a sip of the other. Then he said to Armbruster: "So sorry, old chap, but I've only got two hands you know."

Sir Harry got to his feet, looking daggers at him. He turned to Elizabeth.

"You promised me the next dance, my dear. I shall see you then"—and stalked off.

ॐ

Elizabeth invited Lord George to be seated while they waited for the orchestra to recoup its energies. He was quite pleased to do so and plunged into conversation with her.

"You cannot know how pleased we all of us were to see that Tony's interest has been so aroused."

Elizabeth, her mind still taken up with her recent conversation with Sir Harry, responded: "I am sure Gryfynskepe is not all that fascinating. His lordship has not seen fit to visit it since we came out."

"No, not Gryfynskepe! I was speaking of you, Miss Brown. Tony's bringing you to Claridge's has set us all agog. When is the date?"

"What date?" asked Elizabeth at a loss to follow him.

"Oh come, come, Miss Brown! You can tell me!

I have known Tony from childhood. Why all the secrecy?"

"My lord, you puzzle me greatly. I hesitate to respond only because I do not know what you are referring to. I cannot believe my work at Gryfynskepe can be of any interest to you."

"Your-your *work* at Gryfynskepe? Now *I* do not know what *you* are referring to! I speak of you and Tony. I had thought that you and he had reached an understanding and were keeping it secret. Is it not so?"

"What sort of understanding, my lord?" Elizabeth was not at all happy with the turn the conversation was taking.

"Are you not come to an agreement to be wed?" he asked bluntly.

"No, of course we have not! Whatever put such a notion into your head?"

"Miss Brown, may I inquire where you are from?" Lord George's tone was not at all cordial any longer. Suspicion appeared in his eyes.

"I reside in Bloomsbury, my lord."

Lord George's features went stiff. "Then it is true—what they are saying."

"What they are saying?"

"Er-ah-Miss Brown, you would not by any chance keep a shop there as well?"

Elizabeth, being perfectly at ease with herself, smiled. "Why, yes! I deal in books. If you should ever have occasion to require something in that line, I should be very pleased to assist you, my lord."

"Er-ah-thank you, but I do not read—that is, I-er-can read, but don't! Ah—Miss Brown, I am suddenly put in mind of another engagement and am distressed to have to inform you that I must forgo the pleasure of this dance. I know you will forgive me, for I am late as it is. Another time, perhaps."

He got out of his chair in one abrupt movement and walked quickly away without another word.

Elizabeth was mortified by his action and quite baffled to understand the frigid demeanor he had suddenly adopted with her. It was a shock to her, and it was minutes before she could bring herself to come to grips with this odd turn of events. But she forced herself to disregard the snub until she could come to an understanding of the circumstances that called it forth. As the truth began to dawn, her embarrassment grew and grew until it was transformed into a deep resentment.

It was clear at last what was behind Lord George's ungracious behavior. Tony had failed! He had endeavored to maintain her respectability before the ton. All his efforts had come to nought, and it had turned out just she had predicted. She understood, now, what *they* were saying. She was reputed to be another of my Lord Rakehell's darlings. Now, at last, she had got an explanation for his prolonged absence from Bath.

Oh, how wrong she had been about him! If he could have maintained some respectable facade to cover their connection, all would have proceeded in accordance with whatever plan he had in mind, but it had not worked out and everyone knew her for what she was—a humble shopkeeper—and believed her to be no better than she should be, as was to be expected. Evidently, all that was too much for Tony's proud stomach. How revolted he must be to have his name connected with that of a female, so poor and so low, hardly a prize by any measure in the eyes of the ton—not even as a mistress.

She had been prepared to accept the loss of her good name in this adventure, but to find that she had already been defamed and had not even begun to deal with the marquis was so great a shock to her self-esteem that anger—even rage—consumed her being. The gross unfairness of it all gnawed at her emotions and left her with a sick headache.

It was just as well, for it served her as an excuse to request of Mr. Cowles that they return to to Gryfynskepe forthwith. Neither he nor Mary were particularly happy to oblige her, but they could see that she was in undoubted distress and, accordingly, ushered her from the Assembly Room and down the steps to their coach.

As the coach started off, Sir Harry appeared in the entranceway. On his face was a black scowl.

This unlooked-for departure of his promised partner for the next dance obviously did not sit well with him.

৶

Sunday was a day to stay in bed, or so Elizabeth decided after one look out of her tiny window at the lowering sky and the misted landscape. She was very relieved that they had not stayed on in Bath another day. It was a foul morning, and it quite matched her mood.

Of one thing she was quite certain. Not another parchment would she dust off, not another faded line would she read until she had come to some conclusion as to what she must do.

Mary had arisen earlier and gone down to breakfast, leaving her cousin to sleep. But Elizabeth was too upset to sleep. Everything was out of kilter, she thought. Not a thing was going right. She had gambled everything, and she had lost everything. Now that word had gotten about, she could hardly come back to the shop and resume her trade as though nothing had changed—even though nothing *really* had! For a small fortune in gowns and dresses and a huge debt to the Marquis of Montreat, she had allowed herself to be smeared with scandal and beyond redemption. She was desperate.

She thought fearfully hard and long, trying to determine what she must do. She was as much concerned with her own preservation as she was in finding some way to get her own back at Tony for what he had done to her. But it was very difficult. If she tried to sell off all her newly acquired finery, she would receive but a fraction of what they had cost. In the vast sea of her debt to the marquis, it would be but an insignificant splash. That way was not any solution to the pickle she was in. She pondered and pondered until at last an answer of sorts began to take shape. Slowly a sneer began to spread over her features.

By heaven! my Lord Montreat may have thought it all a great jest, but she would see to it that it was no laughing matter. He had said her fee must be great enough to cover all the expenses she had incurred and more. Well, she would take him at his word! She would apply herself to the work with a vengeance and get through it all. She sincerely hoped that she would find something of value as a result of her search, for it would lend support to the bill she would render, something close to £ 2,000.

Not that she ever expected to see one penny of the money. The marquis was the son of a powerful peer, and he was wealthy and, undoubtedly, power-

ful in his own right. She would never stand a chance
of pressing her claim for services against him; but,
on the other hand, neither could my Lord Rakehell
proceed against her. She would have fulfilled her
commission, and the best he could do was to charge
off her debt to him against the commission. He
would come out ahead, of course, on a pound-and-
shilling basis; but she would have been freed of the
shadow of the Marshalsea, the very thought of that
debtor's hole sending cold chills down her back.

That was what she had to do and she felt relieved that she had that way open to her, but she
was not at all happy over it. She was left with an
ache in her heart, and it was a bitter pain. To be
reckoned one of my Lord Rakehell's castoffs and
never to have known his love for however short
a time was indeed a silly thing to regret, but nevertheless she did regret it and to her everlasting un-
happiness, she was sure.

Mary came in bearing a tray with an assortment
of breakfast meats and some steaming-hot coffee.

"Beth, you must eat something this morning. You
had not a thing at dinner, and you looked poorly
for it."

Elizabeth came up to a sitting position, and Mary
placed the tray upon the coverlet across her knees.

"Thank you, cousin. It was very thoughtful of
you. Indeed I am famished."

"How is your headache this morning? I do believe you are looking better."

"Yes, I am much improved. Well, I shall positively stuff myself and then get back to the work. I think it best we get through it as quickly as we can."

"Oh, Beth, what is the rush? I was saying to Joshua that you had been working much too hard and must have more rest."

"Joshua?" asked Elizabeth. "Pray who is Joshua?"

Mary blushed warmly and looked down at her hands. "You know, Beth! Mr. Cowles. I pray you will not laugh."

"Why ever should I laugh? I will smile. Surely you will allow me to smile for the good feeling I bear you. So now it is Joshua, is it? Our visit to Bath, then, was not a total waste, was it?"

"Did you know he is truly a gentleman—well, he is a younger son. He served with the Lancers in India, but he was not one of the fortunate fellows."

"Fortunate in what way?"

"He never got to be a nabob like so many of the gentlemen in the Indian Service, and he is not at all wealthy as one might think."

Elizabeth laughed. "Mary, you are a gem! You are naive at times, to delight one's soul. I have always had the feeling that Clive was the only lucky one, and all the others had well-lined pockets before they ever went out there. I am sure India is no different in that way than England. To make a fortune, it helps immensely to have a goodly number of pounds to begin with—and that is no guarantee of success either."

"Well, he is not exactly poor. He is paid very well for his service with the marquis and has put much aside. He has an account in the bank right alongside those of the Duke of Verndon and his son, the marquis," she declared proudly.

"Mm-mm! I am impressed! But, my goodness, I begin to suspect the pair of you covered a great deal more ground in the Assembly Room than just dancing. Has he offered?"

"Oh, I would not let him! It is too soon!" cried Mary.

"I have a suspicion you will not be a great deal of help to me in the work henceforth."

"Beth, will you mind so very much?"

"No, I shall not mind. Please to convey to Mr. Cowles my heartfelt approval, whenever you are a mind to."

"Thank you, Beth."

"You know, Mary, while I was lying here, just before you came in, I was thinking how strangely everything has turned out. You came along with me particularly to watch over me, and that has proved pointless. There has been no challenge at all to my virtue."

"You sound disappointed."

"Indeed, I am!" Elizabeth began to giggle. "It is too comical! I was all prepared to defend myself—well, not to the bitter end—but it would have been an exciting contest, I think, and, with you in the wings, I should not have been too easily defeated. I feel so ludicrous that my lord marquis has not appeared, leaving me in sole possession of the field and without a struggle. Truly, my vanity must be greater than I ever realized, to have thought that his lordship had an interest in me beyond the most casual. Well, let it be a lesson to us all. I shall put all thought of him from me and trod the straight and narrow, all thanks to him, God rot him!"

Mary looked shocked.

"Well, that is how I feel!" declared Elizabeth. "And there is nothing like a good oath to express it!"

೪ಿ

It was afternoon and Elizabeth was seated upon a stool in the parchment room, engrossed in perusing a deed to a sixteenth-century holding in Wales. It seemed to have been inscribed partly in English and partly in Welsh, of which latter tongue she had no knowledge. She was trying to determine if she could make out the gist of it and save the trouble of having it rendered into English.

A soft sound behind her made her start and twist suddenly in her seat. She breathed a sigh of relief when she saw it was only Cowles.

"Oh dear, Mr. Cowles, it must be this old horror of a building, but I fear my nerves are on edge that you made me jump so."

"Pray forgive me. I should have given more warning of my coming. I will admit the darkness and the dead walls do not put one in the best frame of mind. Perhaps it is having the same effect upon myself that I come to you with my suspicions. I am concerned, and I would welcome your opinion."

"What about, Mr. Cowles?"

"I left Mary in the kitchen. I'd feel better if you could be there too. I do not like it that you are off in this desolate wing all by yourself."

Elizabeth chuckled. "Do not concern yourself about me. It is not the most comfortable place, but I am sure I am perfectly safe here. You did not have to put yourself to the bother."

He was looking very serious. "I am not so sure. I-I left Mary behind because I wish to discuss something with you, and I fear lest what I have to say will disturb her."

Elizabeth raised an eyebrow. "You believe I am made of sterner stuff than she?"

"Miss Elizabeth, I know you give out to the

world how Mary shelters and protects you, but I have seen it is quite the other way around. Even more remarkable is the fact that I have never witnessed before a female of any rank stand up so well to his lordship as you have—except one."

"I am pleased to know that I am not one poor lone female against the marquis. May I inquire as to who is this other?"

"Her Grace of Verndon, my lord's mother."

"Oh," said Elizabeth, making a face. "I had hoped for an ally. But what is it that you wished to discuss with me?"

"When we first arrived, did you happen to notice a party of workmen at the junction of the lane and the high road?"

"Yes, I did. They appeared to be repairing the roadbed."

"An excellent choice of words, my lady. They still *appear* to be at their repairs, and it is all of a week since we first observed them at it. They have not progressed from the spot."

"I take it that that is unusual."

"I should say it is extraordinary! They are there today—now!"

"Why, it is Sunday!" exclaimed Elizabeth.

"Precisely! I went up to the roof this morning and spied upon them. They are not working. There is not a thing wrong with the road. They just sit and chat."

"Oh dear, that is strange. Would it not be wise to order them to move on?"

Mr. Cowles looked unhappy. "I fear I made a blunder. Instead of spending some time at my post to see if I could determine what it was they were up to, I descended and stood upon the crest of the high bank overlooking them. They saw me and immediately began to nudge each other and nod their heads in my direction. I was too far off from them to hear their words. When they gathered up their tools and marched off in the direction of Combe Hay, I was quite relieved for the moment."

"Why that is excellent! I am sure I should prefer them there than hereabouts."

"Yes, but don't you see? It was very poor thinking on my part. I believe I have confirmed my suspicion that there is something odd about them, but, at the same time, they have been made aware that I am curious. In short, Miss Elizabeth, if they are an enemy—although for what ends, I cannot guess—in a military sense, we have given our position away."

"I do not follow you. They knew exactly where we were from the moment we arrived."

"True—but they are no longer disguised to us. They must be quite sure that now we do not believe they are what they pretend."

"I see nothing wrong in that. If they were up to no good, they may as well believe that we are on to them. Mr. Cowles, I am inclined to think that you are worrying yourself about nothing of consequence. I do not blame you. This place is enough to give anyone the megrims. I know it constantly plagues me with forebodings of impending doom, and it is all I can do to maintain my composure. I succeed only because I keep reminding myself that it only derives from these detestable surroundings, and I shall be happy to see the work at an end and ourselves back in London. Now, I am sure that you and Mary have things to talk about, and I have things to do and would get on with them."

"I am sorry if I have disturbed you."

"Oh, think nothing of it. It is good to talk things out."

Elizabeth was torn out of a sound sleep with a nerve-shattering jolt. Her eyes snapped open, and she found herself straining her ears. She was, at once, wide awake, and her heart was palpitating so that she was hard put to breathe quietly.

She was quite sure that it had been a sound, some great sound that had awakened her, and it must have been something strange and something to terrify, for it to occur at this late hour. Except for the feeble glow of the turned-down lamp on her night stand, it was very dark in the room; and, now, the silence was so complete, it was as though she had lost her sense of hearing.

Suddenly there was a sound of running, trampling feet from below, a door slammed and, from without, there was a shout. It was followed quickly by the noise of horses galloping off into the night. Once again all was silence.

She sat up so abruptly that her bedstead creaked.

"What is it, Beth?" asked Mary in a sleepy voice from the other bed.

"Did you hear, Mary?"

"I heard you stir. Can you not sleep?"

"No, no! I heard something from down below. It woke me, and I do not like it."

"Probably the wind at a shutter. Now, be a good girl and go back to sleep. It must be hours till morning."

"You know there are no shutters to the place—there's hardly any need of them the casements are so tiny—and there is no wind! Mary, I am worried! It is too quiet! Something is wrong!"

Mary sighed and eased herself up. "But, Beth, it is to be expected! It is the middle of the night. Why should all not be still?"

"Because there was something! Sounds of men running and horses galloping away—and a fearful sound that awoke me! After such tumult, this ensuing silence frightens me!"

"Now, you are beginning to frighten me!"

Beth turned up the lamp and slipped out of bed. She began to don her wrapper.

"Where are you going?" asked Mary, suddenly very nervous.

"To see what is wrong. I shall come back directly."

"Well, I'll not stay here alone for any consideration!" exclaimed Mary slipping out of bed. "I am coming with you."

"I'll not be unhappy for your company."

Attired in their night robes, the girls left their bedchamber. Elizabeth carried the lamp and led the way, with Mary clinging as close as she could without tripping on their flowing robes. They came to the head of the stairs, and Elizabeth raised the lamp on high.

The light faded rapidly in the Stygian blackness and they could barely see to the foot. Slowly they descended, the shadows cast by the balusters looming up before them, writing in the flickering light and fading into the darkness behind them as they passed.

In the great room, the lamp was far too feeble to reveal any fair portion of its expanse, and they were forced to make a slow tour of its walls before they could be satisfied that nothing unusual was contained in it.

"Nothing appears to have been disturbed," remarked Mary encouragingly. "Are you sure it was not a nightmare that woke you?"

They both came to a halt before the black rectangle that was the opening to the corridor that led to the rear of the building. It was peculiarly uninviting.

Elizabeth visibly threw back her shoulders. "Let us proceed."

"I am sure we shall find nothing out of the ordinary," said Mary.

"I hope you are right."

"Let us return to our room. In the morning, it will not seem so important."

"No. I am sure something is wrong, and I shall not be able to sleep until I can discover what it is."

Still neither of them set a foot towards the opening.

"Are you so very sure you heard something? I did not."

"I am quite sure," said Elizabeth grimly, starting for the doorway.

"But from whence did it come?" asked Mary, reluctantly following her.

"From below."

"From below? Oh, Beth, not the cellars! Surely you do not intend to go down into the cellars at this time of night. I should not care to visit them even in midday!"

They were now at the doorway and they both paused. Elizabeth lifted the lamp high and peered down the length of the corridor as far as the flickering light would permit. She could see very little and, of that little, nothing was exceptional.

"If we do not find the cause of the commotion on this level, we shall have no choice but to descend."

"Oh no, Beth!" wailed Mary. "Not the cellars! I shall die of fright!"

"Well then, if it turns out that I must go below, do you await me. I shall not rest until I know what is afoot."

Mary's teeth began to chatter. "I-I'd rather n-not! B-Beth, would it not be wiser to awaken Mr. Cowles? I-I should f-feel so much s-safer f-for his presence."

"And I! Where is his chamber?"

"Really, Beth, that is no proper question to ask of me!" Mary exclaimed hotly. "Do you think I should ever be so impertinent as to have asked him?"

"I pray you, Mary, this not a time to go missish on me. If you know, say so and we shall go to him directly."

"I am not being missish and I do not know! Surely it must be behind the kitchen, I should think."

"Amongst the servants? My dear girl, would you have us rouse the house for something that may turn out to have been nothing at all? What a pair of silly fools we should look!"

"Then what are we to do?"

"We had best proceed on our own. I think we should go into the far wing. Reason tells me that if it had occurred near the servants' quarters, they must, all of them, have been aroused. It is as good a place to start as any."

"If you say so," agreed Mary unhappily, "but it is not much better by the parchment rooms than it is in the cellars."

They went through and on down the large corridor until they came to the bend. As they came round it, the rays of the lamp revealed dimly in the distance the open door of the parchment room.

Elizabeth exclaimed: "What is that bundle by the door? I do not recall any such thing!"

Then as they came closer, their hearts faint with apprehension, they could make out that the heap was in fact the body of a man slumped against the wall.

"Oh dear God! It is Mr. Cowles!" cried Mary and she rushed forward.

"Now, Mary, take hold of yourself—!" admonished Elizabeth, very much shaken herself, but Mary was already at his side, kneeling.

"Horrible!" she exclaimed. "His head is all over with blood!"

She began to fuss about him and, as Elizabeth came up beside her, the light of the lamp glittered on the tears streaming down Mary's cheeks.

"He still breathes, thank God!" declared Mary. "Quickly, Beth, summon aid!"

"Yes, at once! I shall leave the lamp with you."

"No, take it with you! I'll not need it!" cried Mary as she sat herself down beside the inert form of Mr. Cowles. Gently she eased him down against her so that his bloodied head and shoulders were supported against her breast. "As you love me, Beth, go quickly!"

Beth rushed off down the corridor.

ॐ

My Lord Marquis:

—I send this to you at Oaklands in the hope that it will find you there or be forwarded to you, and I pray you will forgive me if I intrude upon your pleasures of the moment.

—Mr. Cowles has been attacked and fearfully wounded. His head was quite laid open by his assailants and is now fast regaining his health, so not to worry. He came upon intruders in the night ransacking the parchment room and was sorely wounded when they set upon him and made good their escape.

He has commanded that the coachman and groom mount guard, one with his great pistol, the other with his great sword, and we are all forbidden to leave Gryfynskepe without escort. It is a most grim business and confirms your belief that something of value is contained in that room.

—The Justice of the Peace at Combe Hay has been informed of the incident but, for lack of anything pointing to the culprits, is at a loss how to proceed. Pursuant to my commission, I shall continue to search through the heaps and will inform you immediately anything unusual turns up.

—I write to you not in my own interest and would not have thought to trouble you with our concerns as your continued absence speaks more eloquently than words of your lack of interest in this undertaking. It is only upon Mr. Cowles's insistence that you be informed that I am forced to intrude upon your pleasure of the moment!

—I remain your servant—Elizabeth Brown.

Elizabeth laid down her quill and carefully read what she had written.

Satisfied, she began to fold it up and seal it.

"I do not agree with Mr. Cowles that this is at all necessary. The marquis could not care less."

"Do be sensible, Beth. He is master here and must be informed of what is happening," said Mary.

"How is Mr. Cowles today?"

"Very well indeed. He is up and about. It was not at all as serious as it could have been, I am happy to say."

"To be laid up for three days by some dastard's blow is serious enough by my account."

"Well, yes, I agree. Of course it was perfectly awful, but it is over and he is back on his feet—so it is no longer a cause for further worry."

"Do you think so? I am not so sanguine. I see no reason to prevent the thieves from trying again. Obviously they have the knowledge that we lack. It is fortunate, however, that we are in possession and they are not and so gives some advantage. I know it sounds hardhearted of me, but, in a way, this raid of theirs has *added* to our advantage. It tells us that what we seek *is* in that room. Thanks to Cowles's intervention, they had not gotten to it, for the room was in no way further disturbed. I suspect that they cannot put their hands upon it anymore readily than can we or they would not have had to ransack the other room. It encourages me to continue the search and with all haste."

"But, Beth, how did they get in? All was locked and barred."

"Yes, that is puzzling. Mr. Cowles could find no sign that they had forced their way in."

"But they must have! Really, Beth, they could hardly have had keys to the place!"

Elizabeth turned to stare at her cousin. "You know, I do believe you have hit upon it! Of course they had keys! And it all begins to make sense, too!

Do you recall the peculiar behavior of the Bakers? And the condition in which we found the other parchment room? One is tied to the other, and all are tied to this latest nasty business."

Mary looked surprised. "You say the Bakers put keys into the hands of the raiders?" She paused to think it over. "Yes, I can see that it must be very likely. We have always suspected that the Bakers were hand in glove with someone else."

A look of great interest appeared on Mary's face. "You know, Beth, I am become quite fascinated to learn what is at the bottom of all this. Such persistence, such desperate measures, it makes me wonder. What do you think is contained in that room?"

"I have pondered upon that question often as I scanned the documents and am still very much in doubt. A description or map of some treasure hoard is the first thing that comes to mind."

Mary pursed her lips in doubt. "Don't you think that even Uncle Ethelbert would have recognized anything so obvious?"

"Yes, I should think so. It only adds to the puzzle but, for anything so obvious, I cannot imagine a document that would call for such Trojan measures."

Mary shrugged in frustration. "I cannot think of anything else that would lure a pack of villains and blackguards like crows to a field of corn."

"Nor I. Well, as long as I sit here, we shall get no closer to a solution to the puzzle. The day is young. I should get through a goodly armful before it is time for luncheon."

At that moment, carrying himself with a very martial air, the coachman came to stand in the doorway, his hand resting on the huge pistol in his belt.

"There is a gentleman calling. His card, Miss Elizabeth."

Elizabeth accepted the card and glanced at it. "Oh drat! I am in no mood to receive! It is Sir Harry Armbruster come to call. We were introduced in the Assembly Room, and I left him before he could claim a dance I had promised him." She glanced about with a pained expression. "Well, I do not see that there is any hope for it. We shall have to see him. Show him in."

Sir Harry came striding into the room.

"My dear lady, how very good of you to receive me!" He bowed low. "I feared that I had in some way displeased you that you left the dance so abruptly. If I did, I beg you will accept my heartfelt apologies."

"There is no need for you to feel concerned, Sir Harry. I assure you it was a sudden onset of the headache that necessitated my withdrawal. Indeed, it is *I* who owe *you* an apology for not explaining. Allow me to introduce my cousin, Miss Mary Vernon. Won't you be seated?"

"Delighted, Miss Vernon. Thank you kindly," he responded and sat himself down stiffly, perching on the edge of the chair, his legs thrown out before him in a rather elegant manner. "I am so pleased and relieved to learn that I was not the cause. It did trouble me—But, I say, so you know that your man is armed? I could not believe my eyes! Is there trouble afoot?"

Elizabeth smiled. "I daresay it is shocking; but you see, Sir Harry, we have had some disturbance here a few days past, and it was thought necessary to take steps against a recurrence. I regret if it discomfited you."

"Do tell! Whatever happened? Word of the Bakers' untimely demise is all over Bath, and all would have it that it was lightning that did them in. Do you tell me, now, that it was foul play?"

"Oh no, it has nothing to do with the Bakers. There was an attempt to break in one night."

Sir Harry laughed lightly. "You must be jesting! Whyever should anyone wish to plunder old Ethelbert Quarnell's stronghold? The only thing he had to boast of was his collection of parchment and that, I daresay, he would have had to pay to have anyone relieve him of."

"What you do not understand, Sir Harry, is that—" began Mary.

Elizabeth interrupted her. "What you do not understand, Sir Harry, is that they were just some taverners, quite cupshot, making a fuss. Nothing at all to concern ourselves about in retrospect, but very disturbing when it occurred. Mr. Cowles thought it wise to adopt some sterner measures for our continued security."

"Mr. Cowles? Is he not Montreat's man?"

"Why yes, he is. You have met him?"

"Er—yes. We are not on the most friendly of terms. Er—he did not suffer any hurt in the episode you speak of?"

"He—" but once again Elizabeth interrupted Mary.

"No," said Elizabeth, "not at all. Have you heard otherwise?"

"Yes! That is—I thought—no, I have not *heard* anything to that effect. I was merely surmising that it was a possibility."

"Are you in Bath permanently, Sir Harry?" asked Elizabeth.

He smiled ingratiatingly. "I had not planned to stay there very long, but, if you ladies are going to grace the neighborhood with your delightful presences, I shall not be in any great rush to return to London."

Elizabeth simpered, and Mary, with amazement in her eyes, blushed for her cousin's sudden and strange lack of poise.

Then Elizabeth, appearing all flustered, exclaimed: "Oh dear, I should just love to sit and chat with you forever, but I have so much to do this day that I regret your visit must be so short. Perhaps I shall see you in Bath on the weekend."

Sir Harry got to his feet. "Ah, my dear Miss Brown, if that is a promise, I shall certainly be there and claim the dance you owe me."

"Indeed, Sir Harry, I shall be looking forward to it." She tugged at the bell rope. "I'll have our man show you out."

"That is hardly necessary. I know my way about. Do not trouble yourself."

"Of course. I forgot. Good day, Sir Harry."

"Good day, Miss Brown, Miss Vernon. It has been most charming."

As he stepped through the doorway, the coachman came up and escorted him out.

"Elizabeth, what has come over you?" demanded Mary in shocked tones. "I have never seen you act so—so silly, and before such a fine gentleman. And the way you would not let me put in a word! Really, it was most ill-mannered of you"

"I feared that you would say more than was necessary, Mary."

"I do not understand."

"Please, not now, I beg of you. I must think. And while I do, will you be kind enough to find Mr. Cowles and ask him to spare me a moment?"

"Elizabeth, something is wrong! I know it from your manner. Has it to do with the gentleman who just left? Is that why you behaved so strangely with him?"

"Yes. There is something about the man I do not like. I cannot say what it is for sure, but he rubs me the wrong way. That is why I exerted myself to bring his visit to a close."

"You do not trust him? Is that why you would not let me speak of events here?"

Elizabeth nodded. "Perhaps it was silly of me, but I did not think it was any of his business."

"What do you have against him?"

"Nothing. Not a thing but my own sensibilities —and there is his remark concerning Mr. Cowles. Perhaps *he* can tell us something of Sir Harry Armbruster that may be pertinent to my aversion for the gentleman. Now, go and bring him to me."

"Very well, Beth. But not before I tell you that when even gentlemen callers are to be suspect, I yearn to be away from this place more than ever."

She whirled about and walked quickly out of the room.

In a little while, Mr. Cowles made his appearance, with Mary close behind.

He said at once: "Miss Elizabeth, if I had known your caller was that cad, Armbruster, I'd have never granted him access to you. Where do you know him from?"

"Ah, I was right! Then he is not the pleasant chap he makes himself out to be?"

"Not by a furlong! I know his game. He is very expensive and goes to any lengths to lighten other peoples' pockets. He tried one of his little schemes on the marquis and was caught red-handed. They drummed him out of the club. He is welcome only in the worst of the gambling hells. I daresay even they have become too hot for him if he must spend his time at Bath."

"He is worse than I suspected," said Elizabeth, "and that is cause for us to worry."

"How so?" asked Cowles.

"I was introduced to Sir Harry in the Assembly Room by Lord Richards, with whom I am acquainted through Lord Montreat's offices—"

"Yes, George Richards is a close friend of my lord—but the marquis is bound to have words with him, now. He'll not thank Lord George for introducing you to vermin like Sir Harry."

Elizabeth waved his remark aside. "In any case, we had a pleasant enough exchange, during which he admitted to having called upon Uncle Ethelbert a few times in the past. I thought nothing of it—"

"Was he the cause of your sudden headache?" asked Mary. "I *thought* there was more to it than mere indisposition."

"No, something else occurred—but that is of no pertinence to what we are discussing. Sir Harry was all that was proper, though I was not at all taken with him. But, during his call here, a little while ago, he seemed particularly interested in our business here, and I could not see that it was warranted."

"I am sure it was only idle curiosity on his part, Beth," remarked Mary. "The man was just trying to make conversation."

"I was quite willing to believe that it was no more than that and did not think it at all odd in him until, for a moment, his composure deserted him. His recovery was less than convincing to me."

Mary frowned. "Yes, I recall it. It was about Mr. Cowles having been injured. It appeared to me you were both at pains to hide something from the other. It was most uncomfortable for me because I did not see what there was to hide."

"You see, Mr. Cowles," explained Elizabeth, "Sir Harry inquired if *you* had been injured. He was very specific. He did not ask if *anyone* had been injured."

Cowles thought a moment. With some uncertainty in his voice, he said: "I think I understand what you are driving at, but it is not all that clear to me how it casts any great suspicion upon Armbruster."

"*We* had not kept it secret that you had been injured. Squire Nichols was given all the particulars, and I am sure an inquiry at the tavern in Combe Hay would have been fully responded to in all detail. But Sir Harry seemed to have a wish to approach the subject in a most oblique fashion—as though he wanted to appear completely ignorant of the entire affair. That is why I denied that you had been injured, in response to his query. In his desire to maintain his feigned ignorance, he denied that he had *heard* anything to that effect but had merely imagined it as a possibility. To my mind, he went too far!"

"Ye-es. I suppose one could interpret it thusly— but yet, his denial is not necessarily so unreasonable. He heard of the incident and could see that neither of you ladies were any the worse for it. It was only natural that he should have inquired as to how I had fared. If you thought your denial must have got some rise out of him, why you were out there. For all the fellow's underhanded dealings, he does have the manners and breeding of a gentleman. He would never think to contradict a lady to her face."

"Then you do not think he knows more than he makes out?"

Mary declared: "Cousin, *I* think you are straining at a gnat! Though I can hardly blame you! This place is enough to make one cast suspicion on one's self!"

"Well, *I* am not satisfied. I do not like Sir Harry Armbruster and am convinced his interest in Gry-fynskepe and the raid is more than a passing one."

"Still that is not to say that he had a hand in it,

Miss Elizabeth. I will admit *I* do not wish to see him anymore than can be helped."

"Well, *you* need not, but, until I am convinced that *my* suspicions are groundless, I have every intention of encouraging his acquaintance."

"My Lord Montreat will not like that, I assure you."

"My Lord Montreat can go hang for all I care. If he was here and taking some interest in what we are doing, he might be in a position to determine for himself the merits of my proposal. In his absence, I can see no objection if I proceed in any way I think fit."

"What can you hope to accomplish, Beth? Even if Sir Harry had any guilty knowledge—and I am sure he has not—you would be the last one to whom he would admit it."

"Oh, Mary, sometimes you can be so obtuse! If I were to avoid him, it must only confirm his suspicions that we are hiding something. This way, I have a hope of allaying his suspicions and may even stand some chance of catching him in some greater error than, as I believe, he has already committed."

Said Cowles: "There is one very suspicious circumstance that we must give thought to and that is the fact that our road menders have not put in an appearance since the break-in. I am sure *they* had something to do with it and I am very unhappy if that be true, for there were four of them, and I can only muster three against them in the event they are the thieves and should decide to come against us in force. It was unfortunate that the light was so poor when I was attacked, or I am sure that I would have recognized them as my assailants. I think I had better make application to the squire and insist he provide us with two or three constables to stand night watch."

"We are fast becoming an armed camp. I shall spur my efforts to get through the rest of the parchments just as quickly as I can. The sooner we are done with Gryfynskepe the better, I say."

"And I!" agreed Mary.

My dear Miss Brown: We are concerned to learn of the unpleasantness at Gryfynskepe and hope that there have been no recurrences. My son has directed that you resign your commission at once and repair to Oaklands to render an accounting of your findings to date. By this letter, you are empowered to hire an adequate watch to keep Gryfynskepe secure from plunder. The marquis will arrange for the work to be pursued by someone more fitted to cope with the unexpected difficulties that have arisen.

——His Grace and myself are very curious to make your acquaintance.——Elvira, Duchess of Verndon——

Elizabeth slammed the letter down upon the table and exclaimed in tones of the greatest indignation: "The arrogance of the man! Mary, read this!" she cried, picking up the sheet and thrusting it at her cousin. "He will not even deign to write to us in his own hand, but must hide behind his mother's skirts! Good God! If he is so dissatisfied with my efforts, surely he can turn me out himself and has no need to bring his mother into it!"

Mary read the letter and then looked at her cousin. There was an unbelieving smile on her lips. She said: "Perhaps I might agree but that this mother he hides behind is a duchess. I find it most difficult to accept that a letter of invitation—and that is what it is—from the Duchess of Verndon is in any manner a snub."

"Hah!" sniffed Elizabeth in disdain. "I say it hardly speaks well of Her Grace to be all that anxious to make the acquaintance of her son's latest tart!"

"Elizabeth Brown, what are you saying?!!" cried Mary, shocked to the core. "You are no such thing! Truly, cousin, I do not know what has come over you! How can you possibly take exception to this note from Her Grace? It is purely a matter of business, I am sure."

"It is Tony's business! What has the Duchess of Verndon to do with? 'His Grace and myself are very *curious* to make your acquaintance.' I'll wager they are! They are curious to see to what depths their noble offspring has descended!"

Mary looked very stern. She scolded: "Elizabeth! This is all nonsense and well you know it. Why should their Graces take exception to you at all? There is not a thing between you and the marquis, and I can vouch for it."

Elizabeth conferred a look of pity upon her cousin. "Do you think that that will stand in my favor? My dear, you will only be tarred with the same brush. Do not look at me with so confounded an air, my poor cousin. I know whereof I speak. You recall the headache I complained of in Bath? Well, it arose from this very same cause. My Lord Richards, who I met there, left me in no doubt of his opinion of me. He could not depart from my presence quickly enough when he understood that I was not anyone of note but, merely, a shopkeeper in Bloomsbury. It had been rumored to him that I was and, when I unwittingly confirmed it, it was all that was needed for him to conclude the worst about me, and he is a *dear friend* of the marquis! Can you imagine what all the others must be saying? And do you think that the duke and duchess have not been reported to, in the fullest detail, all about this latest conquest of their son's?"

"But it is not true! You know it is not!"

"What has that to say to anything? My Lord Rakehell has merely to look at a female—any female—and she is forever without reputation!"

"But, Beth, you knew this would happen! I remember you saying—"

"I know what I said! But I never thought for a moment that I should be spurned without ever having experienced-er—"

"*Elizabeth*, I cannot believe my ears! Do you say it would have been better for there to have been true cause for this distressing gossip?"

Elizabeth thrust forward her chin. "Yes, I do!" she retorted. "If I am to suffer these outrageous slings, let it be for good reason or what profit shall I have?"

"What profit shall you have in either case? Oh dear, I knew nothing good would come of this expedition! What are we to do?" she wailed.

"It is not all bad, my dear," said Elizabeth kindly. "Have you not found your Joshua and has he not found his Mary?"

"But you, Beth! What is to become of you? Do you dare to reopen the shop and become a great curiosity to every passer-by? You would die of shame!"

Elizabeth cocked her head and thought for a moment. Then, with a laugh, she said: "Now that is an excellent thought. Of course I shall return to the shop! I should think for a month at least I shall

be a nine-days' wonder, and I'll wager the shop
will do very well while it lasts. As for shame, I
have nothing to be ashamed of." Then her voice
saddened as she murmured: "I wish I had as little to
regret."

Mary sighed. "You are not a sensible female. I do
not know why I ever thought you were. Shall I
inform Mr. Cowles that we are departing?"

"I should say not! We are not leaving Gryfynskepe!" declared Elizabeth.

Mary blinked. "But you are directed to—"

"If Lord Montreat wishes to give me the sack, he
shall have to do it himself. I am sure it is a matter of
sufficient importance that must interfere with his
eternal dallying. What manner of man is he that he
must delegate to another, his mother no less, such
an office!"

"But—"

"And let me assure you that I shall work like three
furies to get this work done before he has a chance.
Then, at least, we shall have some counterclaim to
pose against the debts that I so foolishly let myself
incur."

"But—"

"It is all right, Mary. I shall not ask you to assist.
I think I can go about it more quickly by myself.
I shall resist the temptation of studying each document and go quickly through them my eyes and
mind alerted only to respond to something of out-

standing import—if there is such a thing! So far, I have discovered little of interest to any but a scholar, and that little not worthy of the effort."

"But, Beth, you cannot disregard so completely the Duchess of Verndon. She has requested you to call at Oaklands. You dare not ignore it!"

"I am not ignoring it. I am refusing to comply. I'll not be put on exhibition and, what is more, I have not the least *curiosity* to make her acquaintance. Having met her son, I have got me more than my fill of the entire Quarnell family!"

❧

Day after day for the next three days, Elizabeth devoted herself unstintingly to her task. No more lying in bed until all hours, she was up with the sun and, after the briefest of breakfasts, repaired directly to the parchment room to take up her work.

Before the day was well started, she was reduced to dust and dishevelment, but she gave no thought to her appearance. By evening she was in even poorer case, her eyes burning and a musty odor in her nose and a musty taste in her mouth, but she did not let that deter her. After dinner, she was fain to return to the work and might well have done so but that Mary put her foot down and forbade it, threatening to have Mr. Cowles bar the door to her if she persisted. Elizabeth then would receive a short lecture on how the work was dragging her down and that she must have some relaxation.

And it was true. Three days at the pace she had set herself were just about all that her nerves and her body could stand, and she was forced to moderate the tempo of her labors. It was just as well. As she sat back, finally, nigh exhaustion, and surveyed the room, she could see that she had got through about half of the room's contents. Despite the fact that she still had not come across anything of any worth, she found it definitely encouraging. So long as she could say that she had done, and faithfully, the work for which she had been commissioned, she did not care what she found.

As she looked about her, she realized that she could not proceed further, except with the greatest difficulty. There was now a definite lack of space in the room in which to get around. As she had torn down stack after stack, she had not piled up the rejected sheets in any particular order. Now, the part of the room in which she sat was all cluttered up with a sea of documents, heaped in billows all about and deep enough to prevent access to the stacks farther back.

She stood up smiling at her thoughtlessness. Dusting herself off, she left the room and returned to the kitchen where Cook, who always seemed to be well posted on the whereabouts of the members of the household at any given time, was able to direct her to the small dining room where she found Mr. Cowles and Mary, holding hands across the table and staring deeply into each other's eyes.

They broke apart quickly as she entered the room.

"My dear Mr. Cowles, shall I be calling you cousin soon, or am I being overly presumptuous?"

"Oh, Beth! How odious of you!" exclaimed Mary whose blush, at being discovered tête-à-tête with Mr. Cowles, now deepened more than ever.

Mr. Cowles grinned. "Then you would not object to our union?"

"I asure you, Mr. Cowles, my cousin is her own mistress and not amenable to me in any respect."

"I believe you are being evasive, Miss Elizabeth. Does it not go against the grain with you that I serve Lord Montreat in a more or less menial capacity?"

"I do not see why it should. What have I to be so high in the instep about? If Mary should accept you, then I can be nothing but happy for her. What say you, Mary?"

Between blushing and stammering, Mary was quite beyond saying anything at the moment.

Mr. Cowles chuckled good-naturedly. "By your leave, I should like to do my own proposing—and in my own time."

Elizabeth smiled. "That was bad of me, but I

could not resist it. May I inquire if you have any reservation that you defer—er—popping the question?"

Strangely enough Cowles's features turned quite sober. He looked at Elizabeth with a troubled expression. "I do not expect my lord will be so democratic as you, my lady."

Elizabeth frowned. "The marquis?" she asked.

He nodded.

"What the devil does he have to say?" she demanded, firing up.

Mary gasped. "Beth, your language!"

"I beg your pardon, Mary, but this employer of mine exasperates me beyond bearing. That he should have anything to do with your happiness is not something that I will ever allow."

"You know my heart's desire, Miss Elizabeth. May I rely upon you to speak to his lordship in my behalf?" Cowles asked anxiously.

"If he should presume to interfere—by what right, I cannot imagine—I shall not hesitate to give him a piece of my mind."

Puzzlement replaced anxiety in Cowles's face. "I am sure it need never come to that. He must be guided by *your* wishes."

Now it was Elizabeth's turn to look puzzled. "Mr. Cowles, that is an assumption quite beyond reason, or do you misunderstand the particular relationship that exists between the marquis and myself?"

Mr. Cowles raised his eyebrows. "I had not thought I did."

She glared at him. "Because you are connected with the Marquis of Montreat is no reason why you must look upon me as beneath contempt. I assure you, you are completely out in your opinions. The work that I am doing here is all that is concerned between his lordship and myself, though heaven only knows whether you will believe it. I daresay all of London is quite sure that it is a good sight more!"

Cowles looked to Mary. "I am at a loss to understand, my dear, what exactly your cousin means to say."

Mary shook her head sadly. "Joshua, it-it is too shameful what they are saying. I-I cannot speak of it. It-it is most improper and exceedingly painful to us both."

Cowles eyes narrowed. Then they opened wide. "Miss Elizabeth, exactly what have you heard and from whom?" he demanded with great authority in his voice.

She looked at him in surprise. "Surely, you must have heard?"

"No, I have heard nothing! If it is anything to embarrass you, then it must embarrass my lord, and no one would have the audacity to repeat it in my presence."

"Lest you inform my lord?"

"I assure you, my lady, I am more than capable of protecting my lord's honor as well as his person."

Elizabeth sniffed. "What, against enraged husbands?"

Cowles was taken aback. "Really, Miss Elizabeth, you go too far and do my lord a grave injustice."

"Ah, you would protect his honor here and now, I see."

"That is not what I mean. As he is quite straightforward and never disguises his intentions, I do not see that anyone can take exception to his ways."

Mary exclaimed: "Do you condone his offenses against society?"

"Offenses? Mary, whom does he offend?"

"All respectable persons—and if you do not think so, you are no better than he. Beth, you were so very right. Like master, like man!"

"I say, Mary, this is carrying things a bit far, you know."

"Mr. Cowles, I do not think so and I begin to suspect your intentions."

"Oh, really, Mary, you are being quite missish!" snapped Elizabeth. "I was only referring to Montreat. It has nothing to do with Mr. Cowles."

"I am not so sure," declared Mary primly. "Beth,

I do wish you would finish up here so that we may depart for London on the instant. I have had as much of Gryfynskepe and everyone connected with it as I could care for."

"Miss Elizabeth, what has got into her?" pleaded Cowles.

"I am sorry, Mr. Cowles, but this place is not conducive to clear thinking, I am come to believe. We had best get out of it and quickly. I have been making great progress and would request that you have the loose bits and pieces gathered up and carted off to the other chamber so that I may have room to continue."

There were thunderclouds in Cowles's face as he said stonily: "Very good, ma'am. I shall see to it at once," and he stalked out.

Mary buried her head in her arms and burst into tears.

 ॐ

An anger burned in Elizabeth's breast as she stood looking at what was left to be done. The old chamber was now half-empty, and it was going to be quite easy to get at the stacks of parchment that remained. But she was not seeing them. Her gaze rested upon nothing as her mind dwelt upon the hatefulness of my lord Montreat. So corrupt was he that even as staunch a man as Cowles was blighted by his association. She could have wished that Mary was a little less loyal, a little less prim in her thinking, for she was sure that Cowles was truly disappointed at her rejection of him. And, unlike Mary, she was not so certain that Cowles was anything like the rake his master, the marquis, was. But she could not truly blame her cousin for suspecting the worst of Cowles, considering his exceptional view of his lordship's conduct.

Yet it was a most ridiculous coil! Here was she, ready to give anything at all for the chance of my Lord Montreat's resuming his notice of her, anything at all! And there was Mary, with a good man to hand, sacrificing her happiness for scruples that would be a poor thing to nestle up to down the long years ahead. She sighed. Life became most difficult when one's heartstrings were torn. In the long run, it would be best if she just retired to the shop and shunned all romantic shame.

She walked to the rear of the chamber and began to examine the stacks with a decided lack of enthusiasm. First she touched this one and she ran her hand lightly over that one. She had just about made up her mind to start on a third when she caught sight of something that seemed caught behind the stack against the wall. In the poor lighting it had the appearance of the end of a cylinder.

The neighboring stack was positioned too close to allow her to get her hand in between and, as it was an excuse to delay resuming the work, she began to dismantle the closer stack. As ever, it was dusty work, but it went along quite rapidly as, now, there was plenty of room in which to dispose of the armfuls of sheets. She could not help hoping that this cylinder—as the stack grew shorter and she could get a better view, she saw it was a roll of parchment—might be that which she was engaged to find.

At last she was able to reach it and, carefully, she drew it forth. From its heft, she was assured that it was bound to be different from any other piece in the room. It was somewhat heavier, and the sheet appeared to be thicker.

She dusted it off and untied the ribbon that bound it. As she began to unroll it, she perceived that its thickness was due to the fact that it was comprised of two sheets. Needless to say, her curiosity was greatly aroused, and she was beginning to feel the excitement that comes upon one when the end of the chase is in sight. Her heart was beating rapidly as she got them unrolled and began to scan them.

She understood at once the nature of the documents. The one was a bill of attainder, approved by George I—she recognized the blocky, labored signature of the first of Britain's Hanoverian monarchs—and the other a writ of execution ordered by the

same dignitary. One, William Quarnell, erstwhile
Earl of Sevenoaks, was attainted and ordered put
to death. The date of his execution was neatly ap-
pended to the writ. She knew what they were but
was puzzled to understand their significance. She
pondered for a while before resuming her study of
them.

It was quite puzzling. Sevenoaks was the present
seat of the Quarnells, and one could assume that the
duke listed amongst his holdings that of the earldom
of Sevenoaks; but, if his ancestor had been attainted,
how could that still be? The law of attainder would
have called for the forfeiture of all the earl's holdings; nothing could pass to him from his predeces-
sors, nor from him to his heirs. She frowned.
Something was not right at all.

She wondered if the bill could have been reversed
by one of the Georges subsequently, restoring all
the Quarnell's rights and privileges—little could
have been done for William, of course, but at least
his heirs would have come into their own, as seemed
to have happened. But that is what puzzled her.
Such a proceeding, the reversal of a bill of attainder,
would have been a most noteworthy event and,
therefore, to someone like her, the name Quarnell
must have been emblazoned upon her memory.
Bills of attainder were rare enough now that the
monarchy was so well established. Their reversal
must have been even rarer. But she had not known

the name of Quarnell until recently, and then it was only in connection with a notorious debauchee—but how, then, could the Quarnells still be occupying titles and holding properties that had been stripped from them unless it had all been reversed?

She put that point aside for the moment and gave her thoughts over to the assumption that the Quarnells' holdings were not legally theirs by virtue of these documents she held in her hand. At that, a wicked smile lit up her face. Oh, how delightful a prospect! Tony Quarnell, stripped of his wealth and his title—a mere commoner such as herself! Where would his arrogance be then? What of the duchess' "curiosity" to meet her? Oh, how marvelously things would be changed! What a lift to her spirits to be able to spurn with impunity that insufferable, black-garbed, cock-a-hoop of a marquis!

But Elizabeth could not deceive herself. Spurn Tony she never could, be he ever so humbled and impoverished; but she was sure she would have preferred him so, for then, perhaps, she might deal with him as she could never do so now—with him so high and she so low.

She stared off into space and absent-mindedly brushed away a lick of hair that had fallen over her eye. Her lips tightened as she considered that these documents must have a consequence to the Quarnells such as she imagined, and somehow she must come to an understanding of exactly what they meant.

She recalled that Montreat's reason for engaging her was that he could trust her. Yes, if these documents spelled ruination to the Quarnells, he certainly must count trustworthiness as a prime qualification, indeed. She did not dwell upon the possibility that she might betray that trust. Her task was to find whatever was of value, and she could not say whether or no this find was what it seemed to be until she had thoroughly studied all the facts concerning it, so she told herself. That was excuse enough to refrain from informing my lord for the time being.

But it *did* have to be valuable! How else explain the attempts to rummage through the stacks by the nocturnal visitors. And, carrying along on that line of thinking, she was reminded of her suspicion of Sir Harry Armbruster. If she was correct and Sir Harry was associated in some way with the attack on Gryfynskepe, then he must know for sure what this was all about.

Yes, that fit the facts, and her suspicions were almost become a certainty. There had been no further disturbances. Sir Harry had made his call for the purpose of determining how the household had fared. When he saw that they were armed and on the alert, of course he realized that forcible entry was now ruled out. That was why he was interested in maintaining his acquaintance with her. She was to be his key to the documents.

She reviewed her conclusion and could see no fault in it. She resumed her seat on the stool and smiled. Suddenly things were turning out to be most interesting and, she thought, to her advantage.

Sir Harry had the information she required, and she had the prize which he sought. Betwixt and between them there was bound to be a way to put this to her own advantage. If she went about it cautiously, she just might be able to learn from Sir Harry his interest in the documents and still keep the documents for herself if their value warranted it.

She did not fool herself into believing that Sir Harry was not a dangerous person to have to deal with. Obviously he had confederates in his employ who thought nothing of stealth and violence, and she had the distinct impression that their leader was not at all behind them in resorting to desperate measures. Yes, she would have to have her wits about her if she was to gain her end and keep herself out of harm's way.

And then what? Suppose it was all as she suspected and hoped—that the Quarnells had no right to their estate and rank, what then?

She shrugged as though to unload a burden from her shoulders. She'd worry about that when she was sure that there were real consequences to require it.

Her mind came back to Armbruster. How did the man fit in to the puzzle? What was his interest? What need had he for these papers? What did he intend doing to secure them? And, if he was the plotter whom she suspected was behind it all, then he must be willing to risk upwards of £10,000 to gain his ends. That was what Tony had been offered for the property in excess of its value. It gave her pause. That was a sum to tempt better men than Sir Harry, and it could be but a fraction of the stake that Sir Harry must envision.

But one thing did not fit and, upon it, her conclusions snagged and bid fair to go all to pieces. It was Tony's attitude. He was so negligent about the entire business. Obviously he was interested but not even enough to take the trouble of coming out to Bath as he had originally planned.

Did he have any idea of what it was that he had engaged her to find? Quite possibly he did not. It was not logical that he would trust *any* stranger with so fearsome a secret. Surely his first duty to his family and himself was to see such documents destroyed, never giving anyone a chance to even hear of their existence, much less take possession of them. But where was he? How could he have stayed away at such a critical time? A sense of righteous anger arose within her. If he had been present, she would have given him a thorough shaking for being such a reckless noodle. Here, in her hand, could well be the tools to bring his whole world crashing down about his ears. No, he could not be so stupid. It must be that he had not had any idea of what was hidden in Gryfynskepe.

Well, the long search was over, and now she must begin her efforts to determine exactly what it was that she held in her hands. Until she was ready, no one must know about her find, and she would have to keep the old documents well hidden.

Where to put them was something she now had to consider. She just might return them to the place where she had found them. No, that was not a good idea. This room must still be the target of anyone interested in searching, and the documents must be quickly found now that so much of the contents of the room had been removed. That consideration brought up the notion that, as the other room was already filled to overflowing with discarded parchments, it must be the very place to keep her prizes perfectly secure. No one would think of looking there and, even if they did, all she need do was to slip them under the others at a spot she would mark well.

She arose from the stool and rolled the two parchments up in reverse to straighten them. Then she went down the hallway to the other chamber and, observing the ruined door hanging drunkenly ajar by one twisted hinge, she smiled in satisfaction. It was the perfect guardian.

Glancing up and down the corridor to make sure no one was approaching she slipped inside and deposited the uncurled documents just under the peak of a small hill of discards. Marking the location in her mind, she sighed with relief, dusted off her hands and skirt and departed to find Mary.

ॐ

As she came to the point where the narrow corridor turned into the broad one, Elizabeth encountered Cowles looking sober to the point of sullenness.

"Ah, Mr. Cowles, I had hoped to find you! Will you be kind enough to escort us into Bath tomorrow?"

He scowled as he replied: "If it is all the same to you, Miss Elizabeth, I shall have Smithers drive you in. It is my duty to keep watch over matters here and, in light of recent events, I had best not be absent from Gryfynskepe."

Elizabeth wrinkled her nose. "I see that Cousin Mary and you are still out with each other."

"I am sure that that has nothing to say to it! Miss Mary is entitled to her opinions, and I have my duty to perform. Since I am sure you must be of a mind with her, you can only be relieved if I stay behind at Gryfynskepe and out of your sight."

"Mr. Cowles, my cousin does not speak for me, nor may you! As to your duty here, if I am right —and I am sure that I am—there will be no further break-ins, especially if I get to Bath this weekend."

"How can that be?"

"I am very sure that Armbruster is involved— even behind it all. His coming to call was for no other purpose but to scout out how we were getting along. He could not have failed to discover that we were prepared and that any further adventure could never gain his objective but could result in serious losses to his forces, even if we ourselves did not come out of it unscathed. Sir Harry may be rash as to principle, but I think he is not foolish."

Cowles could not forbear a smile. "Indeed, Miss Elizabeth, that is a most soldierly estimate of the situation. I am almost convinced that you are right. But pray tell me how does your going to Bath help to insure us against further assaults?"

"What Sir Harry can do, so can I. Since military parlance can express it so nicely, let us say that I am going to Bath to reconnoiter and see if I cannot get from the enemy the knowledge that we need."

"Do you really think you can? Suppose you are completely out in your surmise and Sir Harry is not our man."

"Then I shall have lost nothing but a few boring hours in his company."

"Well, I do not see that you will require my presence for any of that."

"Mr. Cowles, it is just possible that I might make a slip—I am not so conceited as to think I am letter perfect in such an endeavor as this, and it is not beyond the possibility that the enemy may proceed against me in force. I should feel ever so much better to know that there was a reserve at hand."

Cowles chuckled. "How you do go on! My late colonel could not have put it better. Very well, I shall escort you ladies, but I doubt if Miss Mary will be pleased."

"I do not agree. Where is she now?"

"In the dining room and all storm clouds."

"Thank you, Mr. Cowles. Perhaps I can let a little sunshine in. Heaven knows there is too much gloom about as it is. By the way, has there been any further word from his lordship?"

"No, my lady, I should have informed you immediately had there been."

"It does not surprise me."

"I hope you will pardon me for saying so, but I would point out that as his lordship is expecting you at Oaklands—"

"Oh, bother his lordship! His place is here with me—with us! We have serious business afoot, and it would not kill him to leave off, for once, his eternal dalliance! Do not speak to *me* of what his lordship expects!"

"As you wish, my lady."

"And you will please to cease calling me 'my lady'!"

Cowles bowed and walked away.

Elizabeth proceeded to the dining room where she found Mary huddled in an armchair in a corner of the room. She could see that her cousin had been weeping but affected not to notice.

"Mary, we are going to Bath tomorrow."

"Well enough! Anything to put distance between us and that odious man!"

"That odious man has promised to escort us."

"Then *I* shall stay behind!"

Elizabeth drew up a chair alongside her cousin and sat down.

"That you shall not! I have got to speak with Sir Harry Armbruster in private, and I can hardly do so with Mr. Cowles at my elbow."

"Then take Smithers. He can stay with the coach."

"No. It is possible that there is some risk in this business, and so long as it is known that Mr. Cowles is in attendance it will help to abate it."

"Do you mean to say that you want *me* along just to keep Mr. Cowles entertained? Oh, Elizabeth, how bad of you! After what that man has said, I could never trust myself to be alone with him, ever!"

"That is utter nonsense and I think you carry things too far when you allow it to destroy your chance for happiness! Surely you cannot believe that Mr. Cowles is cut from the same cloth as the marquis! Because he is devoted to his lordship does not necessarily mean he subscribes to his lordship's ways nor does it mean he follows in his footsteps."

A light of hope dawned in Mary's eyes. "Oh, Beth, do you really think so?"

"Has Mr. Cowles been anything less to you than a perfect gentleman in any way since you have known him?"

"No-o," replied Mary hesitantly. "But, for that matter, has Lord Montreat been anything less than a gentleman with you?—and we all know what he is!"

Elizabeth burst into laughter. "My dear Mary, you do not know it but you have proven my point! Now you can be perfectly at ease with your Joshua, for I can assure you that my Lord Montreat, at our very first meeting, behaved towards me in as loathesome a manner as you can imagine."

"What do you say!" exclaimed Mary, her eyes wide open in amazement. "And you can still fear to lose your heart to the creature?"

"I have already lost it and am now suffering the consequences."

"Oh, you poor dear!" said Mary, tears welling up in her eyes.

"Mary, enough! Or you shall have me bawling like a babe, and that I do not need. That I am a pea goose is my own concern. I never doubted that he would break my heart, and there it is. He has done it and much sooner than I expected. That is no reason for you to share my pain. Will you come with us to Bath?"

"Yes, Beth."

"Then go seek out Mr. Cowles and apologize to him. You have caused him a great deal of unnecessary pain."

Mary, in great dismay, cried: "Oh, Beth, I could never be so brazen!"

"My dearest Mary, it is high time that you tried. You do want Joshua, do you not?"

"Yes," she murmured.

"Then it is up to you to let him know and in no uncertain terms."

"But if he does not want me?"

"At the very worst, you will suffer an embarrassment, a small risk when you consider what it is you are hoping for. And anyway, it is no risk at all, for it is not up to him to refuse you, you little fool. It never is. It is always up to the fair sex how it shall go. If you go about the business in the right way, you cannot fail. You are mature enough to appreciate my meaning, I think, without my having to spell it all out for you."

Mary gave thought to this idea, her face brightening perceptibly. Obviously, she wished to be convinced. But then her face clouded over with doubt.

"Beth, if that is so, why do you find *yourself* in such fix? Surely if it would work for me, must it not work for you as well?"

"Oh, let us say it is the exception that proves the rule!" she exclaimed with impatience, but she thought better of it and went on. "No, that is not fair of me to dismiss it so casually. One must be sensible about it, and I daresay I was not. One must put a limit on one's hopes. I was not sensible on that score. Even from the beginning I knew that Montreat's interest in me was nothing beyond the usual for him, yet I proceeded to build such dreams upon it that I blush to recall. You pointed it out to me. It was too obvious. But that is not anything like the case with you and Joshua. Surely you must see it and act accordingly."

"I understand and—and will do as you advise. But what business do you have with Sir Harry?"

"I suspect that he knows more than he has said, and I am determined to discover it. I am sure it will assist me in my search by affording me some indication of what I am looking for."

"I see. Well, I am going to find Mr. Cowles." She got to her feet, thrust her shoulders back and walked from the room very purposefully.

Elizabeth slumped back in her chair, biting her lip. She was quite displeased with herself for not having told Mary about her discovery. She had never excluded her cousin from her confidence before.

&

"We are well met, Miss Brown," remarked Sir Harry after they had exchanged greetings. "Have you come alone?"

"No, Sir Harry. My cousin and Mr. Cowles make up my party."

"Ah—you know if you had not come, I should have been forced to seek you out at Gryfynskepe."

"La! How very flattering! I am overwhelmed by your interest."

Sir Harry regarded her out of narrowed eyes. "Miss Brown, I wonder if I may be frank with you?"

At that point, Elizabeth regretted very much having left her fan behind. It was just at such a moment she could have used it to some effect to simulate a fluttery female. She did the best she could by putting her hand to her mouth, turning her head coyly away and simpering: "Oh, Sir Harry!"

He retorted impatiently. "It will not do, Miss Brown! I have been at pains to study you, and I am sure that playing the shy maiden is not your forte. Moreover, I interpret this play-acting to mean that you are dissembling. I have a very strong impression that you know a great deal more than you care to let on."

"I haven't the vaguest idea of what you mean!" replied Elizabeth, feigning surprise.

"Then I shall explain it to you. There are all sorts of rumors current about you, Miss Brown—and, I daresay, most of them are far off the mark. I know for a fact that you keep a shop in Bloomsbury— books and that sort of thing. By your own admission you are engaged upon a confidential business for Montreat, and it requires your presence at Gryfynskepe. I believe it to be so and scoff at all reports that there is anything more between the marquis and you. Believe me, Miss Brown, I am quite familiar with the sort of females that Montreat amuses himself with, and you are not in their style at all. Having come so far in my thinking, I can readily discount your attempts at coyness. They will not wash for, if Montreat's interest with you is purely business, it must follow that you are highly qualified and must be accounted a serious-minded body, otherwise he'd never be concerned with a female of your appearance and station."

Elizabeth's face flushed with anger. "Your delicacy of expression leaves something to be desired!"

"I daresay, but I have no time for the niceties and must insist upon calling a spade a spade."

"Very well, then, I shall deal a few cards myself!

I have strong reason to believe that, despite your denial, your interest in Gryfynskepe is more than mere idle curiosity. In fact it is specifically directed to the work I am engaged in, to the extent that you did not hesitate to resort to force to get to the prize before I did. Be warned! Such an attempt, if repeated, will be foiled and your confederates laid by the heels. But I am sure you already have observed that we shall not be surprised again."

For a fraction of a second, Sir Harry's eyes opened wide. It was the only sign he gave of having been startled. He stared at her. Then he smiled coolly.

"I see, Miss Brown, that I have grievously underestimated you and Cowles. You are quite right. The attempt will not be repeated. I am all out of confederates. When they came limping back to me, all torn and bloody, I had no recourse but to pay them off and turn my thoughts to other devices, especially when I learned on my visit to you that Cowles had not suffered in the melee. I had no idea he could make such headway against what I had every reason to believe were my superior forces. But, of course, he told you how he had damaged my coves. The craven blackguards had the nerve to claim that they had done for him. If they *had* at least put him out of action for a time, I might have been tempted to try again."

Elizabeth chuckled in a superior manner. "Well,

I shall certainly have cause to commend Cowles to his lordship. I had no idea he had wrought such devastation amongst your forces before his head was laid open," said Elizabeth, smiling shrewdly.

"Then it was a pure bluff on your part!"

"Aye, it was. I had my suspicions even then. I am pleased to see how accurate was my judgment of the situation. You may feel quite easy about the state of Cowles's health. He is now completely recovered. I know how much you are concerned for him."

The barb struck home, and he grinned in acknowledgment.

"Indeed, Miss Brown, you are a foeman worthy of my steel."

"Sir Harry, when my Lord Montreat arrives—and we expect him at any time, now—you may well find yourself in danger of being completely outgunned."

"No, I think it will not be that way—and that is not because I believe myself capable of withstanding two such formidable opponents, but rather because it will not come to that. You have an excellent head on your shoulders and will know wherein lies the greatest profit. In short, Miss Brown, although I had hoped to outwit you, now I am anxious to help you to the end that we both may gain great wealth at small risk."

"You are taking a risk even now, Sir Harry. How

can you be sure that I shall not turn you over to the authorities? You have fully incriminated yourself to me."

"Other than your own word for it, you can not supply a smidgin of proof."

"I daresay that an investigation will bring to light that it was you who offered such an exorbitant sum for Gryfynskepe. What more is needed?"

"I say!" exclaimed Armbruster. "Montreat must place the highest reliance upon you to have told you about the offer. I sincerely hope his trust is *mis*placed. Nonetheless, it is still no proof of anything illegal. I am not to be trapped so easily—"

Elizabeth laughed scornfully. "Do you honestly believe that Montreat would require more than that knowledge, coupled with my word, to do you the greatest harm? Do you think he is a man to be bound by the doings of courts and justices? If you were in his place, would you ask for more proof?"

Sir Harry suddenly looked very unhappy and took out a handkerchief to mop his brow. Elizabeth was pleased to see that she had got him on the run. This interview was turning out better than she could have hoped. She made no further comment. She did not think she would have to. She was right.

Bravely, Sir Harry declared: "You know you are speaking nonsense. You have no intention of doing such a thing, or why do you stay? Because you wished to give me ample demonstration that I do not have a green girl to deal with, I am sure. However, when it comes to shrewdness you will not find me so lacking in that department either. I am persuaded that your object in coming to Bath, today, was not for a holiday, but to confront me. And why? Certainly not to see me taken in charge. You have an ulterior purpose in all this, and I have found you out. You are after the same thing that I am and for the same reason, but you have not been successful in discovering it because you do not know exactly what it is you are looking for. You have deduced from my interest that I *do* know and have come expressly to seek my assistance. You cannot persuade me it is otherwise."

"Indeed, Sir Harry, you are every bit as perspicacious as I took you to be. Now, the thing I wonder about is, Are you wise enough to realize that even though I do not have my hand on the parchment—you cannot deny it is a parchment we are looking for—I shall ultimately come into possession of it?"

He bowed in agreement. "You need say no more. I understand perfectly. Permit me to suggest a stroll over to the Parade Ground where we will find a secluded spot to insure our privacy. I have the knowledge that will be of assistance to you, and I think you will be quite interested to listen to certain suggestions I wish to make."

She nodded and, taking his arm, they walked slowly away.

ঔ

Off to one side of the Parade Ground there was a huge overhanging oak. It was under its leafy shade that Sir Harry conducted Elizabeth. It was a private retreat and had the further advantage that any intrusion would not occur without significant notice, since anyone approaching could be easily seen. They seated themselves upon a small bench, and Sir Harry began to speak.

"It was perhaps three weeks before the old gentleman passed on that it all began. Being in the vicinity and having some small acquaintance with him, I elected to spend an evening at cards with him at Gryfynskepe. He appeared to welcome my visit and was about as cordial as one might expect. After experiencing a supper of meager proportion and crude preparation, we began the business of the evening.

"Mr. Quarnell was an excellent hand at cards, but he was not all that sharp. I, on the other hand, am also excellent at cards and not at all above being sharp—"

"So I have been given to understand," said Elizabeth with a chuckle.

He smiled. "I have Cowles to thank for that remark, no doubt. Well, to proceed.

"I shall not indulge in false modesty and assure you that at cards I have no equal. Admittedly I am not the very best at playing a hand, but when it comes to manipulation—Ah, that is quite another suit indeed."

Elizabeth remarked offhandedly: "But even at that you are not the best, I have heard."

He frowned in annoyance. "My dear Miss Brown, even the best of us cannot be in top form all the time. That night at play with Montreat was just one of those times."

"I see."

There was something in her tone that made him look at her. She was giving him a wry stare.

He dissembled his irritation with laughter. "You are not about to be bammed even a little. Very well then, I will admit the profession lost a great performer in Montreat. If his hands were as dexterous as his eyes are sharp, there would be few to match him. He caught me and, I tell you, for the longest time, I was hard put to find play anywhere. As a matter of fact, that is why I was reduced to finding my way to old curmudgeons like old Quarnell."

"But if your circumstances were so reduced, how

could you have bid for Gryfynskepe—and for so much?"

"As you will come to understand, a day or two more of my having access to the place, and it would have been the Quarnells who'd have paid—and handsomely. But let me proceed."

"That was your first mistake, Sir Harry," remarked Elizabeth.

Immediately, he grew hot with indignation. "Really, Miss Brown, I may have underestimated the situation here and there a bit, but to state that I made a mistake—"

"My dear Sir Harry, had you offered a third of what you did, my Lord Montreat would have suspected nothing, and you would have had clear sailing. As it was you overplayed your hand with your fantastic bid and, it can be safely said, even a greener hand than Montreat could not help but wonder at it. That is what brought me into it."

"Blast me! Am I losing my touch?"

"I should not be in the least surprised, but I shall reserve judgment until I have heard the rest of it. I tell you now that, at this moment, I am not overly impressed."

He looked extremely annoyed, and she wondered if she had goaded him too far. He fumed a bit and cast unfriendly looks at her, but that was all. The fact that he continued with his recital told her that she had the upper hand and that he knew it.

"To make a long story short, suffice it to say that by the end of the evening, old Quarnell was behind to me some £400. I assure you, had the stakes been reasonable it would have been four times that figure."

"Enough of your bragging, Sir Harry. You are beginning to bore me."

He took a deep breath and continued. "He pleaded poverty and suggested a way to untold wealth if I forgave him the debt. Ever willing to entertain such a prospect, I encouraged him to proceed. He claimed that given a little time, he could place in my hands the key to the Quarnell fortune. He had in his possession a bill of attainder and a writ of execution upon William Quarnell, a traitor during the time of George I, that somehow the family had suppressed, and—"

"Now how could they have done that?"

"Very good of you to ask. I did so myself. This Earl William had been involved in a Jacobin uprising in the North. He had been captured and brought to execution, one of many at the time, coincidental with George ascending the throne. The Quarnells had spent fortunes to have it all hushed up and stricken from the records. But for the confusion attendant upon the change in the ruling house, they might never have succeeded. As it was, the name William Quarnell was never heard again in the land. The only evidence that remained was the original document which, fortunately for us—and others—was never destroyed, as originally intended. Quarnell, you know, was the son of the late Duke of Verndon's second wife, a Spendor, and it was his claim that it was the Spendors' possession of these very documents which paved the way for that marriage. Quarnell claimed he was more a Spendor than a Quarnell, and he guarded the documents with his life to insure that the Quarnells never dared to disown him.

"He went on to say that he was too old and sickly to make use of them and as he had no descendants they were of no use to him. Naturally, I requested to see them, but he informed me that they were very well hidden and he would have to go to some pains to bring them to light. He bade me be patient. All he would say was that they were secured in the rooms he had set aside to store his collection of documents, and no one but himself was ever allowed to enter either of them.

"Now here I did commit an error and do admit it. I should have stayed on to collect my debt, but, being woefully short of the ready, I went off to Bath where I had such a run of good luck I quite forgot for a while the business at Gryfynskepe. The news of the old gentleman's death brought it all back to me, and I hotfooted it to the old ruin only to find Montreat already in possession."

Elizabeth nodded. "So you bided your time, suborned the Bakers, and began to rummage through the rooms. You had completed one and were just starting the other when circumstances—namely Cowles and myself—prevented you from proceeding further."

He grinned. "Precisely."

"Now it is my turn. Obviously it shall be I who finds this bill of attainder, and you cannot prevent me. Pray tell me exactly how you plan to use it."

"Surely I do not have to tell you that." He gave her a queer look.

"If we are to work together, I think you had better. There must be no room for misunderstanding between us. I daresay that our ideas are not too far apart, but, as you are bound to have given it a great deal more thought than I, your plan may be better in detail."

"Now that there are two of us in it, of course there has to be some revision, but it is quite simple. In fact I should go so far as to say it is an improvement. You see, one of us retains the document while the other approaches the Quarnells and dictates the price they will have to pay out if they wish to acquire it." He laughed villainously. "Wish, did I say? Why they will beg me for it! With the loss of their titles and their estates staring them in their faces, what choice do they have? It stands to reason that this third George, being a Hanover to the bone, would never let such a plum escape his plucking.

I shall be perfectly safe from them, for you will have the document and they dare take no measure against me other than accede to my demands."

"How far were you intending to squeeze them? Their titles are not transferable, and I should think their estates could not be appropriated without comment."

"Quite, but there are funds, and there have got to be investments readily convertible to gold to line our pockets. They will have to sell out those. I have little love for Montreat as you know, and it is only just that he will be the hardest hit. In actual wealth that can be made available to us, his is the greatest share, for the duke's holdings are mainly in land, buildings and so forth."

"He'll not be so arrogant after we have done with him," mused Elizabeth.

"Ah, I see he has had his effect upon you too. He has spurned you, has he not? Foolish girl! You should have known! But it is all for the best. It is well that our feelings concerning my lord, the marquis, run neck and neck. It will steel us to our purpose—if that were necessary." He gave vent to a nasty bark of laughter.

"I do not believe anything will be served by continuing this conversation. It is probably wise if we are not seen much together. Be assured, Sir Harry, as soon as I have got my hands upon the document, I shall send you a signal. I am in complete accord

with your plans, and you have my consent to proceed. Although it would be a good thing if we could
trust each other, it would be foolishness beyond
consideration to believe that we can; therefore,
know that I shall not produce the document until
the funds can be paid over and we share them on
the spot: seven shares for me and three for you."

"What! Here, here, now! You go too fast, Miss
Brown!"

"I think not. You cannot do a thing without me,
but I am not so bound. I can easily find another
confederate—and probably not have to part with
more than a share—or, if I put my mind to it, accomplish the matter completely on my own. But I
am impressed with your grasp of the situation and
your address. I believe that you have a proper feeling for this sort of negotiation and am therefore
willing to be generous. In proof of which I came
to Bath, today. If you think about it, you will realize that, other than enlisting you for the reasons
I have just given, there was no real need for this
visit."

He smiled sourly. "Ah, you are a cool customer
indeed, Miss Brown, and I must admire you. Perhaps after this bagatelle is over and done with, we
might cast our lots together. We could go far together, Miss Brown."

"That is something that has not escaped me, Sir
Harry, you may be sure."

"Excellent!" he exclaimed suddenly in very high spirits. He rubbed his hands together vigorously. "I shall await your word."

"Good day, Sir Harry."

ᕲᕲ

Elizabeth remained standing beneath the great tree, her eyes unseeing, fixed on the vast expanse of the Parade Ground. Now that he was gone, her self-control was shattered all to pieces by the great sense of shame and the deep feeling of revulsion that flooded over her, bringing her to the verge of tears. She shuddered, sick with disgust at what her interview with Sir Harry Armbruster had revealed of him and of herself. She trembled from the sheer relief of having managed to carry it all off so well.

Oh, it had been the easiest thing for her to envision how *she* would deal with my Lord Montreat if possession of the bill of attainder conferred such power upon her, but it was quite another thing entirely to find that so base a scoundrel as Armbruster had thoughts not so very much different than her own. The idea that Harry Armbruster should ever have Tony at his mercy was not a thought that she could live with. That *any one* should ever have Tony at his mercy was as unthinkable. She could never go through with it and that she had even though she might now filled her with guilt. She was no better than Armbruster and she had despised that man.

No, the entire plot was revolting to her sensibilities. If the Quarnells were not entitled to their station, it was not any of her business to call them to account. In fact, she did not see that it was anyone's business at all.

William Quarnell had paid for his perfidy with his life. She could not see that justice would be served any better by extending the punishment to his descendants. Furthermore, it had happened at a time when the reigning house of the Stuarts had been denied and their heritage passed on to a foreign Teutonic family: The Hanovers, English not by grace of God but by act of Parliament. She held no brief for either party in that dispute but could well appreciate how a man of those times might well have been confounded to know his true king.

No, not Elizabeth Brown, not Harry Armbruster, not anyone would be permitted to bring the Quarnells to their knees if she had anything to say to it—and, thank heaven, she did! It was all in her hands and only hers. The very first thing she must do was to see the documents, both of them, destroyed and as quickly as possible. She did not trust Armbruster to sit idly by.

With that resolve, she pulled herself together and

strode quickly back to where she had parted from
Mary and Joshua. She smiled to think of them.
There had not been the slightest difficulty in getting
them back together again, and she was proud of
herself for having accomplished it. It had not taken
anything beyond the effort of getting Mary to
speak to Joshua. He had been more than willing to
respond.

It was the one bright ray in this otherwise miserable sojourn. She had come to hate the sight of
Bath. Bath, where my Lord Montreat had promised
to meet with her, was now double anathema to her,
associated as it must ever be with the malicious face
of Sir Harry Armbruster. She had not a wish to
continue her stay. As soon as she got back to Gryfynskepe, she would see to the documents. They
should be easy enough to burn. Then it would be
back to Bloomsbury to try to pick up the threads
of her life so hopelessly raveled and torn by Tony's
heartless intrusion upon her peace of mind.

But, when she came upon Mary and Joshua
seated at a small table, joined in warm conversation, their hands touching, the thought came to her
that life in Bloomsbury could not be the same for
long. Mary must leave her soon. There could be no
doubt upon that score, and she would have to
brace herself for the loneliness that must then be
her portion.

She came up to them, announcing: "We had best return to Gryfynskepe."

Immediately, there were objections. She had been at work so hard and so long she needed some diversion. They had but just got there. There would be dancing later, and what a shame to miss out on it. Gryfynskepe could wait.

She turned a deaf ear to it all and insisted that they return at once. She would explain when they had got back. For now, she just wished for time to think, and she could best do that as they drove.

This caused a spate of inquiries, to all of which she refused to respond. She did say that she had spoken with Sir Harry Armbruster and now must give consideration to what he had said to her and to what he may have implied, for they were bound to agree he was a sly one, and one must step carefully with such a slippery fellow.

Mary and Joshua, both very disgruntled, allowed her to browbeat them into acquiescence. They returned to their carriage and started off for Gryfynskepe.

છ

They had not passed through Combe Hay when Elizabeth, who had been pondering on the various new aspects of the situation all during their progress, gradually became aware that her solution did not seem so satisfactory as she had deemed at first. If she did destroy the documents, would that be enough? What was there to stop Sir Harry from carrying out his part? She could not doubt that he was smooth enough to pretend to have the documents and convince the Quarnells of it. Until it came time to produce the bill of attainder, he did not need her or the documents. By then it might be too late. He would not hesitate to use force to secure the wealth that they would have amassed for the purchase of the documents.

Once having destroyed them, she would be powerless to stop him. Without their existence, the Quarnells could hardly risk believing her assertion that they had been reduced to ashes as against Armbruster's claim that he had them. In short, the burden of proof would be upon her. She could see that she had no choice. The documents must be preserved and surrendered to the Quarnells. Only then could Armbruster be foiled.

She did not like the idea. There was always the risk that Sir Harry might tumble to what she planned and risk a raid to wrest the documents from her. To forestall him she would have to move quickly. But then, the next question was even less easily answered.

Where was she to move? How was she to go

about seeing that the documents were placed into the hands of the Quarnells? Was she to go up to Tony and present them, with a curtsy, saying: "See what a good girl am I?" and be dismissed with a pat on the head? Rather she would have liked to have cast them into his face and cried: "Be damned to you, sir!" Well, neither was at all likely. Where was Tony? She could just see herself roving all over England, with Sir Harry hot on her heels and those confounded documents always at her side, trying desperately to come up with the marquis. Ridiculous!

And, really, just how clever was his lordship after all? Could she be sure that he could be made to understand the import of the bill of attainder and the necessity for keeping everything quiet until it had been destroyed? Bah! She would not trust the business to anyone but the titular head of the house of Quarnell, the Duke of Verndon, himself. There was the chance that he might not even be as clever as his son, but, at least, since he rarely left Oaklands, he'd be a deal easier to locate.

As she pursued this line of reasoning, the rational part of her mind experienced great difficulty in accepting all those postulations and surmises as making any sense. She found that she was floundering in a welter of uncertainty and, perforce, made an effort to clarify the matter in her mind.

One thing came out quite clearly. She had a very

deep sense of guilt over having come so close to betraying the Quarnells to Armbruster, and it interfered with her ability to consider the matter from a disinterested point of view. How was she to face the Quarnells? She was not some child caught with its hand in the sweetmeat jar. She was a base and contemptible person who had plotted the depredation of a family which, through the agency of its scion, had trusted her to carry out a task in confidence.

She was well aware of the fact that she could never have carried off her pose of fellow conspirator with Armbruster if, for the moment at least, she had not been hand in glove with him. With this thought to haunt her, she did not see how she could surrender the documents to His Grace with any aplomb at all. Certainly, she could not face Tony! If he were to but look at her the slightest bit askance, she knew it would all be up with her. She must break down and confess her villainy and understand that the sight of her in his eyes must be loathsome. What an odious turn of events that must be! She would have lost every chance of ever seeing him again.

This last chain of thought impressed her with the desirability of getting out to Sevenoaks and completing the business with the duke before Tony had any chance to get wind of the matter. Not that that would make it all so much easier, but, at

least, she would be spared seeing Tony's contempt
for her.

No, it was too much to ask of her! Better to put
a light to the old parchments and watch them curl
up into black, brittle cinders—and, at the thought,
all her doubts came rushing back upon her. By
the time they drew up before the great stony mass
of Gryfynskepe, she was as much at a loss what to
do as she had ever been.

ॐ

For the next few days, Elizabeth closeted herself
in the parchment room and went through the pretense of continuing her search. It is doubtful that
she absorbed anything at all of the contents of the
sheets that passed through her hands, for her mind
was dreadfully disturbed. She was no longer sure
of anything at all. It seemed to her that the world
she had known was fast coming to an end. Just
days ago she believed she had so much to look forward to and now, suddenly, it was all over with
her. She had lost her reputation, she had lost her
heart, she had lost all taste for the shop, she had
even lost her good conscience. But worst of all was
the realization that she had never had the slightest
claim on Tony and, when she handed over the

documents to the Quarnells, the meager tie that had existed between them would be dissolved in a manner that would never suffer it to be renewed.

She had no wish to let the affair go on to the end which she knew she must. If she could have, she would have made time stand still, but it was rushing by and she was pressed to leave Gryfynskepe. Sir Harry would not be patient for long and soon must begin to wonder why he did not hear from her. She must be away before he took action. She could not afford to face him again.

It had taken all her resolve to carry out her ruse the first time. Now, weak female that she was, she was far too distraught to fool even a child. Her emotions were in a constant turmoil, and the tension within her had never left her since that last day in Bath.

Oh how she had changed—and in so little time! She felt old and weary. She felt life was not worth the candle and wished she could hie herself over the Channel to the South of France and put all these tribulations behind her. But that would take money and she had none. Somehow the distant future would have to take care of itself.

For now, the days were passing, and Sir Harry's visage came to occupy an ever-growing prominence in her mind. It was abundantly clear that only at great risk to the Quarnells dared she tarry at Gryfynskepe any longer. But where to go? She

dreaded having to call upon their Graces at Sevenoaks, but she knew that sooner or later she must.
She decided better later. Perhaps once she was
home again in Bloomsbury, it would all sort itself
out into a neater bundle, one she could cope with.
Gryfynskepe had always been the poorest place to
get any thinking done.

Thus it was that on that very afternoon she came
forth from her self-imposed Coventry and an-
nounced that she had finished her task. She informed
Mary and Joshua that she had found nothing and
could see no good reason for not returning to London at once. She had taken the precaution of
secreting the two documents beneath the clothes
and accessories filling the large handbag she generally carried with her. There were no objections,
and things were quickly put to order, including the
installing of a watchman-caretaker. By the time
darkness fell, they were well beyond Bath, rolling
along the road to London.

ॐ

The very next morning after their departure, Sir
Harry Armbruster presented himself at the door of
Gryfynskepe, feeling somewhat put out at Miss
Brown's tardiness in informing him of the expected

discovery. When he learned from the watchman that the entire party had fled, he was more than put out, he was quite furious. He did not stay to wheedle his way within to explore the parchment rooms because he had no doubt that he would find nothing of value. Miss Brown's departure was all the signal he required to understand that she had found the bill of attainder and, more, that she had abandoned him.

Now Sir Harry was rarely ever made a fool of and, when it did happen, he was not the man to back off and nurse his injured conceit. He had greater spirit than that, and the very fact that it was a female who had gulled him added so much more fuel to the fury that was now consuming him. Although it was become too late for him to garner the fat prize for himself, he would have his revenge by seeing to it that she did not profit from it either. He put his mind to work as he let his horse amble back towards Bath, and it did not take him long to see exactly what he had to do.

If he calculated things correctly, why the very people she hoped to harm would become the instruments of his vengeance upon her. He smiled as he ran through his scheme in his thoughts again. Yes, it was an excellent idea, for he was fairly sure that the Quarnells would see him well paid for his warning. Aye, he would take the whole tale to Oaklands. Forewarned, the Quarnells would be well armed to deal with Miss Brown in a manner she least expected. He might even be more fortunate. If the Quarnells chose to silence her in a particularly permanent fashion, he would be happy to oblige them with his silence so long as he could live off his knowledge of the bloody deed in comfort for the rest of his life. That would be a perfect windup of the affair. It would be so much more convenient for him, too. He preferred blackmail to extortion, though not many would have understood the niceness with which he distinguished the two. Ah, how perfect to pull complete victory out of what must have surely been total defeat!

He put his spurs to his horse and cantered back to Bath. She had a start on him, but not by so much considering she was traveling by coach. He was sure he could reach Oaklands before she did if he hurried. He eased his horse into a brisk trot as he came into Bath, but he did not stop. He continued on through, passing his hotel without a pang. He was on to more important matters and could not waste the time to settle his score there. And, in any case, the few pounds remaining in his pocket would not have made much of an impression on his bill for lodgings. He did not think either he or his host would have much profit if he stopped to bid him farewell.

He came out of Bath and settled down for some hard riding. It was a long ride he had before him, and he was bound to take every advantage of the roads, lanes and paths that would bring him to Oaklands before Miss Brown. He did not hesitate to strike out across country, and he completely bypassed London. By his reckoning he was sure to get to his destination a full day ahead of Miss Brown's coach no matter how fast she ordered her coachman to travel.

On the afternoon of the third day of weary bouncing in the saddle, Sir Harry came into Sevenoaks. He stopped at an inn there just long enough to refresh himself for his visit and remove from his clothing as much as he could of the stains of travel. Of course his wardrobe was far behind in Bath, so he could not change. Allowing himself a half hour, he was finally satisfied he would make a reasonable appearance, and he started off for Oaklands.

He was not kept waiting long and soon disappeared into the interior of the great house for upwards of an hour. At the end of that time, he reappeared, walking with some difficulty. The reason for his odd gait was that a tall and burly gamekeeper had him by the nape of his neck and the seat of his unmentionables, forcing him to quick march with a queer skip reminiscent of a jumping jack. This strange form of leave-taking came to an abrupt end just outside the great door. At that point the heavy hands released him, and a great

booted foot swiftly moved up to contact him somewhere to his rear with such precision and such violence that he was sent flying out to land all asprawl
upon the graveled path.

The gameskeeper stood silently at the door, legs
apart, arms akimbo as though waiting for Sir Harry
to make one small move in the wrong direction.

But Sir Harry had not the least intention of doing
anything but put all the distance he could between
himself and the Quarnells. His swollen jaw and his
blackened eye undoubtedly had something to say
to his decision. He got unsteadily to his feet, dusted
himself off and went to his horse. Getting astride
of it, he rode off without once looking back.

He had told his story in some detail and had not
spared Miss Brown. At its end he was assisted into
a temporary state of unconsciousness by means of a
smarting blow to his eye, rapidly followed by a
crunching smash to his chin. When he came to, he
was invited to leave for distant parts lest his blood be
on the hands of the Quarnells. Since the invitation
was accompanied by a walletful of notes, he accepted it with great dignity. Even though he lost
all of that dignity shortly afterwards as has been
seen, he was very happy to be out of it, especially
after what had been spelled out for him. And, too,
he had the great satisfaction that when Miss Brown
did arrive, her reception would turn out to be far
worse for her than his had been for him.

ॐ

About the time Sir Harry was embarking upon a vessel bound for Australia—the memory of more than one set of fierce Quarnell eyes had led him to believe that the far side of the world might be just far enough from that formidable family to insure his continued good health—Elizabeth and Mary were saying farewell to Joshua Cowles at the door to their chambers in Bloomsbury.

"Are you for Oaklands, Joshua?" asked Mary rather anxiously.

"No, my love. I've no idea where his lordship is and will proceed to his residence in town. I have a strong presentiment that I shall have to bring it to order if he is not there. You know what servants are these days."

"Wi-will I be seeing you then?"

"Lord love you, Mary! Every day, I promise you," and he reached out his arms for her.

"Joshua, not with Beth standing by!" she admonished him.

Elizabeth let out a chuckle. "I pray you will not mind me—but stay! A minute of your time and I shall withdraw. Joshua, do you have any of my lord's money remaining?"

"Oh, I beg your pardon, Miss Elizabeth!" He fumbled at his belt and drew out a generous sheaf of bank notes. These he made to hand over to her.

"Oh, no!" cried Elizabeth. "I have no need of so much! Just a few pounds will do."

"Miss Elizabeth, it is all yours. I am not empowered to withhold any of it from you."

"Oh, very well. What are a few hundred pounds more or less when I already owe thousands. Thank you, Joshua."

"Thank you, my lady. It is a relief to be rid of it. When one has hopes of marriage staring in one's face, a sum like that is a very great temptation."

"In that case let me relieve you of the temptation." She pelled off four £10 notes and handed back the rest, some seven hundred pounds. "With my blessing and with a wish it will speed you both to your happiness."

"Oh, never, Miss Elizabeth! My lord would skin me alive if I accepted such a gratuity."

"It is not a gratuity, you cabbagehead! I hope your wife-to-be has more sense. Mary, you take it."

"But what am I to do with it?"

"I could not care less what you do with it, so long as you take it. At least, then, *you* will have gotten some profit of all this mess I have brought you into. Take it, Mary, before the wolves come ravening down upon me."

Both Joshua and Mary together cried: "What mess?"

"Never mind. None of you is concerned in it, Joshua, I pray you will look after Mary in my absence. I shall be better for knowing that you will."

"Of course I shall, but where are you off to?"

"Yes!" exclaimed Mary. "What is all this mystery? You look positively haunted. We have only just returned. I cannot think of a thing to call you away and so soon."

"It is something I have to do—and by myself. I suddenly realize that I cannot let things continue a minute longer without supplying the remedy. I thought I could put it off, but I am worried that delay will only make matters worse. As I am still packed, I might as well leave now."

"I do not like this, Miss Elizabeth. It sounds to me that you are in some sort of difficulty. Pray allow me to assist you."

"I assure you, it is nothing that you, or anyone, can help me with."

"But you are entrusted to me!"

"For once, my dear Joshua, I must countermand your master's instructions. You must see to Mary, and you cannot be in two places at once. Refer my lord to me if he should make any complaint. Now, good-bye and fare you well!"

With that she picked up her bag, walked quickly

to the stairs and stopped. She turned, waved as she smiled, and descended, quickly passing from their sight.

Mary looked troubled. "Something is dreadfully wrong, Joshua, and I do not have an inkling. Did you see how sadly she smiled at us?"

"I do not like this at all. My Lord Montreat will like it even less."

"There is nothing you can do. Beth is quite headstrong and will have her way."

"She puzzles me greatly. I have not the faintest idea what her way is but, at one time, I could have sworn that it was in the identical direction with my lord's."

"I do not understand you, Joshua."

"Oh, it is nothing to trouble your head about. The next time I meet with his lordship, I shall ask him to inform me if I was mistaken. But I would give a great deal to know where she is off to. I am damned if my lord will like it the least bit!"

By nightfall, traveling post chaise, Elizabeth arrived in Sevenoaks and put up at the inn. It was an excellent hostelry. The service was all that was courteous and thoughtful. Her supper was very well prepared and served. Her room was ample and the bed comfortable. There was not a hint of mustiness, showing that the place was kept well aired.

For all its excellences, Elizabeth did not spend a

good night there. The thought of what she had got to face on the morrow disturbed her rest to the point that she got very little. Their Graces of Verndon appeared to be personages distinctly unfriendly to her. The duchess' letter to her, she recalled, had distinctly struck just such a note, and if she had to judge the duke by his son—which was her only clue to him—then he must be formidable indeed. Tony had proven himself a cold and heartless being. Without a qualm he had dragged her down into the mud. She sensed that the frigid note of "curiosity" in the duchess' letter was a reflection of how badly she had been prejudged. No doubt Tony had been embarrassed by having his name coupled with hers by gossip and confirmed for his parents their worst opinions of her in his charming way. She writhed inwardly at the thought of the undisguised contempt that would be her share as she forced herself to lay the documents before the duke and explain their importance to him. Chances were that he would not credit her because of her lost reputation. If she had the wits God gave her, she would have been wiser to have handed the parchments over to Joshua and kept her skirts clear of the Quarnells. Why in the world had she not?

She thought about it on and on during the restless night and could only come up with the explanation that it was her duty to do so. She had come within a hairbreadth of betraying the Quarnells, and it was only just that she undertake the task as some sort of penance so that she would thereby restore her own good opinion of herself. She would never admit to herself that she hoped Tony would be there because she still feared to have him discover her near perfidy. So it was with torn and conflicting emotions that she greeted the dawn and roused herself from her dreary bed to prepare herself for the ordeal at Oaklands.

She dawdled through her toilet and lingered over her breakfast to make the time pass. She did not wish to appear on their doorstep so early in the day as to make her reception even more cool than she expected it to be. It was coming on to ten o'clock when she decided it was time.

She had attired herself in a sober walking dress, taking great pains to appear as neat and prim as possible, making doubly sure that her front was not in the least revealing. Whatever they might *think* of her, she was bound and determined not to look anything *like* it.

She came out of her room and went to consult with the innkeeper with regard to transportation out to Oaklands.

"That is most easily arranged," he said. "I pray you come with me."

He led the way out to the roadside and approached a large, richly appointed coach. On its

ghly varnished door panels was emblazoned a de-
ce in which trees and acorns were liberally
isplayed. One glance was all she needed to rec-
gnize the Quarnell coat of arms.

She shrank back, causing her host to turn to her.
Is something not to your taste, Miss Brown?"

"I would not wish to impose. I prefer to hire my
wn vehicle."

"But that is nonsense, my dear lady. This is the
uke's very own carriage. His man is waiting for
ne arrival of some expected company. I am sure
ney would be quite happy to carry you as well. I
o not err in taking you for a gentlewoman, Miss
rown?"

"No, you do not err—"

"Then there can be no objection. The duke's
oachman is instructed to carry callers to Oakland.
Ie is a most hospitable great gentleman and would
e much distressed to learn that a guest was put to
ne inconvenience of hiring her own transport out
o the estate."

"My dear man, as I am not to be a guest of His
Grace's—you see, I am not expected—I should be
nposing if—"

"Here you, Fred!" he shouted.

One of two men, dressed in livery, standing at the
eads of the lead horses, looked up. In his hand he
arried a whip.

He nodded, said a few words to his colleague

and then came over to the landlord and Elizabet[h]

"Fred, this lady has a need to visit Oaklan[d] but, because she is not expected, hesitates to go [in] the duke's carriage. I am trying to persuade h[er] that it is perfectly all right for her to do so."

Fred Coachman studied Elizabeth for a momen[t] "May I ax yer name, ma'am?"

"Brown, Miss Elizabeth Brown. I—I wish [to] speak with His Grace but he does not know me— that is, he is not acquainted with me and he do[es] not expect me."

"I begs yer pardon, Miss Brown, but His Grac[e] does expect ye. If ye'll kindly step aboard. . . ." h[e] said, gesturing to the equipage.

"But how could he have?" exclaimed Elizabet[h] startled. "I only made up my mind to come ou[t] yesterday afternoon."

"I know nothin' o' that, ma'am. I only know as how I was to come inter Sevenoaks each da[y] until you come. This be the second day and them be me orders."

Very unsure of herself, Elizabeth allowed her self to be helped into the coach and in a short whil[e] they were off, the other servant, a footman, takin[g] his post up behind.

It was a very pleasant drive and a most luxuriou[s] one, too. It reminded her of the marquis' coach that she had used so much at Gryfynskepe excep[t] that it was even more opulent. The Quarnells di[d]

ot stint themselves for accommodations on the
oad.

When she observed that they were approaching
ne gates of the estate, she gathered up the roll of
archment preparatory to dismounting, but the
oach wheeled right on through with barely a
hange of speed and went rolling right along. She
at back, thankful for the slight respite.

She tried to relax by telling herself that perhaps
would not be the ordeal she feared it would. If
Tony was not there to witness it, she was sure that
he could maintain the businesslike front necessary
nd get it all over with quickly. After all, she was
loing them a service, even if somewhat belated.
There really was not that much to be done. She
ad merely to surrender up the documents, make
ure that the Quarnells understood what they
ignified and suggest that they dispose of them in
onfidence. She had only to maintain herself deaf
nd blind to any contempt they might show her and
eave. That would be the end of the business. Yes,
hat would be an end to the business and every-
hing else, she thought bitterly.

She gave herself a little shake and looked out the
vindow. They were passing through a thick oaken
vood. It struck her that she was seeing where
Tony, as a child, must have romped and played,
nd it gave her a warm feeling.

The wood thinned out abruptly, and the drive

traversed broad, well-tailored, rolling lawns fc
some time. At last the coach began to slow as
followed a long sweeping curve. In the distance,
great mansion loomed up. Its front was high, an
the great white pillars supporting its massive ped
ment conferred a majestic look to the whole.

The coach drew up in front of it, and the foo
man came round to help her down. For a momen
she found it difficult to stir. The house and its vas
park bespoke such wealth and power as she ha
never imagined. For the first time, she was begin
ning to understand the great distance that separate
Tony from her, and she wished devoutly that h
had never come into her life to stir up such hopeles
wishes in her breast.

"Miss Brown, we have arrived. If you will pleas
to follow me . . ."

She made the effort and got down out of th
coach, clutching the parchment roll to her. The tal
servant led her into the house and showed her int
a small study off the great entrance hall. Requesting
that she wait there, he withdrew.

It was a small room, well lighted by large tal
windows overlooking the green expanse of th
lawn. For all its lack of size, the room was richly
appointed. The writing table had silver implement
and a leathern letter case upon it. One wall wa
lined with books and the windows with draperie
of a light stuff, drawn back so that the soft light

eflected from the lawn, filtered in. It was a very
restful sort of room, and it contrasted with the
mounting turmoil in her breast.

Never had she felt so out of place. Never had
she felt so lost. What business had she with such
great people? She would have been far wiser to
have told Mr. Cowles the entire story and given him
the documents to dispose of. Maybe it was not too
late! Maybe she could yet slip out and return to
London. It was a ridiculous thought—and anyway
it was too late. She could hear someone approaching.

ॐ

A tall, silver-haired gentleman stepped inside the
room and stopped. Reaching for a lorgnette
dangling from a ribbon about his neck, he lifted
it to his eyes and proceeded to examine her with a
haughty arrogance that was very reminiscent. His
manner informed her that this must be His Grace
of Verndon and she was very disappointed. All she
could see in him of Tony was his manner and his
height. Beyond that he was of massive build where
Tony was slender and was generally fair where
Tony was dark. Not even about his eyes was there
any similarity to Tony, especially as they were

blue and Tony's were a dark brown, almost black

The haughtiness of his manner was in his tone as he said: "I am Steven of Verndon."

"I am Miss Elizabeth Brown, Your Grace," she said as she sank into a deep curtsy.

"Young lady, has no one ever told you that you overdo your curtsying? I am not of the blood royal, you know."

It was the very voice and manner of Tony, even to the thought expressed. At once she began to feel more at ease with him.

She smiled up at him and replied: "Yes, Your Grace, I have been told."

"Then why do you not mend your manner?" he snapped.

"This is but the second time in my life I have had occasion to exchange words with ranking nobility."

"It hardly matters. I doubt if you will have further occasion for it where you are headed."

There was an undisguised threat in his tone and it shook her.

"I—I do not understand what you imply, Your Grace," she said blankly.

"Before we have done, you will understand and quite clearly. Never doubt it, Miss Brown!"

"Your Grace, I realize that I may be intruding on you, and I know that my business with you is not of a pleasant nature, yet I am baffled that you should have taken so unmistakable an aversion to me at this, our first meeting."

"Be assured, young lady, it is our first and it shall be our last. As to my aversion to you being unmistakable, how could you expect it otherwise when the business that brings you is so very unpleasant? But, however unpleasant it is for me, for you it shall be a far sight worse than unpleasant when I have done with you."

Elizabeth was plainly baffled. She could see no reason at all for the duke's attitude.

"I hope, Your Grace, that you are misguided as to who I am and will come to understand that the unpleasantness is one that I have come to help you remedy. Until you know in what peril—"

"Stop your nonsense! You do not fool me for one minute! Your scheme has been discovered to me, and all that is left is to give you your choice of punishment."

"Punishment! Surely, my lord, you mistake me! And you frighten me so that I-I am at a loss to understand you. Pray, let me tell you of my business before you misjudge—"

"Gad! You are a cool one!" he exclaimed. "Misjudge you indeed! Young lady, in my day there were ways to handle such as you as to leave you in no doubt of the evil which you plotted. This is an easier age, and it is going out of style to flog you through the streets before carting you off to Newgate. Do not look at me with such round-eyed innocence! If you but knew how your very presence tries my patience! Ah, that is better! You are frightened now, and truly. Well, you should be! To come here on such business should fill you with shame! Bah! I doubt if the word is in your vocabulary. Miss Brown, I have not the temper, the patience nor the time to bandy words with you. If I stay another minute, I know I shall not be responsible for your health! Wait here! I shall leave you to more patient hands then mine—and more merciful. Thank your stars, Miss Brown, that it is not up to me to deal with you as I would! But do not thank them too much for your doom awaits you nevertheless!"

With that he strode from the room, leaving Elizabeth all atremble. She had not the vaguest idea what it was all about and could only continue to believe that some horrible mistake was being made. If she had been uneasy before she had ever stepped foot in this house, now she was properly terrified and panic filled her breast.

She went over to the window, full of apprehension and struggling in her mind to convince herself that, somehow, she would come out of this all right. Once she was given a chance to explain her reason for calling, they could not but believe that there was no harm in her. She stared out upon the lawn and worried what it all could mean—and

how Tony felt about all this. Surely, he must know
that she was not evil and he must tell them so. Before she had come, she had hoped he would not be
present; now she devoutly wished that he was about.
A few words with him and all this rage and fury
at her must be quickly dissipated.

A small sound behind her made her start. She
whirled around clutching at her breast in terror.

Standing a few paces from her was a smallish
woman. Her deep, dark eyes immediately put Elizabeth in mind of Tony as did the fine lineaments of
the little duchess' countenance. The peeress was
petite but nonetheless imposing. She was staring at
Elizabeth, a coldly disapproving look in her eyes.
Elizabeth felt extremely uncomfortable.

"You have every reason to be frightened, Miss
Brown."

Elizabeth tried to stand her ground. "I do not
know why I should, Your Grace," she retorted.

"I see you have a wish to play your game out to
the bitter end. I warn you it will be most bitter—
for you! But, if you insist, I shall accommodate you
for as long as my patience will allow. Let me say,
before we begin, that you are grievously ill-
matched for it."

"Your Grace, I do not wish to offend—"

An acid smile spread over the lips of the
duchess.

"—but I have no understanding at all of what His

Grace was inferring—and I do not know what you mean by 'game.' "

"It is merely a conceit to describe this little effort of yours. It is very much like a playlet except that its purpose is so vicious."

Elizabeth could only stare blankly and shake her head.

The duchess sighed. "Alas, I can see we are going to be at it a little while. Please to be seated. Would you care for some refreshment?"

Elizabeth sat down and shook her head. For the moment, she did not trust herself to speak.

"Now, then, what is your business with us?"

Elizabeth began to unfurl the rolls of parchments. Very carefully she straightened them out and offered them to the duchess.

With a look of dusgust Her Grace accepted them, glanced briefly at one and, again, as briefly at the other, nodded, and carelessly tossed them to the floor.

"How much, Miss Brown?" she asked, her lips tightly pressed together.

"Your Grace, I beg you will not treat them so cavalierly," protested Elizabeth. "Can you have the slightest notion of their import to the Quarnell family?"

"I may not have the expertise on bills of attainder that you lay claim to, Miss Brown, but I understand hese well enough to know their true worth. How much are you asking?"

"I am relieved to hear you say so." She sighed. "I am pleased to be rid of them, they are such a grave responsibility. You will be sure to destroy them, Your Grace? I'd have done it myself but thought it best that it be done by the Quarnells."

"How much, Miss Brown? You still have not said."

"My fee has already been paid, but—"

"Indeed it has, but not at all to your liking! That was a most excellent performance. Unfortunately, you have missed your cue."

"My cue?" asked Elizabeth.

"Yes. You see your confederate collected the pittance we considered his services worth, and I daresay it was a deal less than either of you expected. Now we shall see to it you are served in a like manner."

"But I have no confederate. You speak as though I had committed a crime!" exclaimed Elizabeth in great dismay at having suddenly found herself plunged into confusion again.

"I see no need to drag this out any further, Harry Armbruster has been and gone, and he left us with the complete tale of your plotting against us. Indeed it was all very well thought out, and I give you credit for that. It even might have worked to your advantage except that these parchments are, pure and simply, forgeries, Miss Brown!"

"But they cannot be! I examined them most carefully. The ink is faded just as one might expect, the parchments of an age. The first George's signature is unmistakable. I even took pains to examine the seals and I can assure you they are genuine—or a most perfectly executed copy. . . ." Her voice trailed off in consternation.

"I am sure you are right—a most perfectly executed forgery, Miss Brown, not a copy."

"H-how can you be so sure, your Grace?"

"There never was a William Quarnell. The names have alternated between Steven and Anthony as far back as the Quarnell genealogies go and that is well beyond the time of George I. Now will you admit the game is at an end?"

"Do you say that it was I who forged these—"

"No, not at all. You merely have had the misfortune to be caught in another's trap. It is quite simple. The late Mr. Quarnell, as you know, had a love for old parchments but, what is more, he prided himself on his ability to create them as well. We have no doubt that he was irked by Armbruster's gouging him at cards and resolved to pay him back with these spurious documents of his own manufacture. I imagine the old chap must be whirling in his grave with joy over how well his scheme worked. Needless to say, we are not overjoyed

hat he saw fit to involve the name of Quarnell in
is jest, but there it is. His sense of humor was as
trange as the life he elected to lead. And so we
nust ring down the curtain upon this tragicomedy.
Comedy for us, tragedy for you, Miss Brown."

"Your Grace, I assure you I had no intention of
oining in with Sir Harry. I believed these parch-
nents to be genuine—"

"Enough, Miss Brown. Your protestations cannot
oossibly serve you. You are caught red-handed and
nust suffer the consequences. You shall be served
no differently than your confederate, Armbruster.
Will it be Newgate by yourself or Australia with
your accomplice?"

Elizabeth sat stunned. Yes, it truly was at an end,
out such an end as she had never contemplated. She
had been charged and convicted as a malefactor and
now was being sentenced for what was really another's attempted crime. It was incredible that anything like this should be happening to her—but it
was, and she felt powerless to prevent it. Her mind
struggled to understand how it could have turned
out so very badly for her. It was not much of a
truggle. As her mind cleared from the shock of it
all, she began to understand.

Armbruster had discovered her departure and immediately assumed she had gone to carry out the
extortion on her own. He had rushed down to
Oaklands to beat her to the prize, only to be

tripped up by the nonexistent Earl William. Uncle
Ethelbert had got back his own on Sir Harry and
in the process, she was caught up in it just as badly
It took no great stretch of the imagination to pic
ture Sir Harry, once caught in the toils, casting as
much of the blame as he could upon her innocen
head so that they might go more lightly with him
Oh, what a horrid fix she was in. What could she
say in her defense? How could she prove herself
against Sir Harry's accusations?

"I hardly think I have offered you any choice a
all, Miss Brown. Why do you take so long to make
up your mind?"

"It is not the choice that is so difficult, Your
Grace. I was only taking a few moments to ponder
on how it all turned out this way. I never thought
that anything could become so strangely twisted."

"Felons never do, Miss Brown. That should be a
lesson to you as you make your way to Australia."

"Australia! Never, Your Grace! If I must choose
let it be Newgate!"

"Surely you jest!" exclaimed the duchess. "In
Australia you can start life afresh. Only disease
and death await you in Newgate."

"Yes."

"Yes, you say! Do be sensible, Miss Brown. We
have a wish to punish you, not to order your ex
ecution. You are still young. I insist you go to
Australia!"

"No, I shall not go!" declared Elizabeth adamantly.

"What have you against Australia, may I ask?"

"I have nothing against Australia except that—that it is so far. I will not leave England."

"But there is nothing for you in England—only disgrace."

"Yes, I know that. But if life can prove so false, I have had my fill and want no more of it. You know, I still cannot believe this is happening to me. My downfall is so perfectly contrived no one would ever have believed it was possible, surely not I. I am completely without defense. I am sure I cannot open my mouth but you must believe me to be as base as ever. It is a horror to know that I cannot look to anyone for succor and must accept this unjust doom supinely. The irony of it all is that I cannot blame Your Grace for doing this awful thing to me. If I were in your shoes and had to judge from these appearances, I must do as exactly as you are doing. It is pointless for me to struggle against it."

"Now you are being sensible at last."

"Is-is Tony—I mean Lord Montreat about?"

"Why do you wish to know?" asked the duchess with suspicion.

"I hope he is not. I shall be taken away in chains, shall I not? I could not bear to have him see me so."

"How very touching, Miss Brown, and you with a lover on the high seas bound for Australia!"

Elizabeth came erect and stared directly into the duchess' face. "I have no lover nor have I ever had one!" she declared firmly.

Her Grace challenged her. "Do you deny that you and my son—" She stopped. Elizabeth had let out a little cry and completely dissolved into copious weeping before her astonished eyes. Suddenly, this cool young woman, who had not flinched at the sentence passed upon her, was reduced to tears for no apparent reason.

The duchess was not at all satisfied. Until this moment, the scene had progressed just about the way she had thought it would. The girl had been faced with her guilt and had made a show of protesting. That was to be expected. Well, her protests *could* have been a bit more dramatic. In fact, if there were to be tears, that was the time for them, not now! Something was decidedly not right in Her Grace's opinion, and the matter before her was too serious that there should be any doubt. This Elizabeth Brown had not the look of a low conniving female, and Her Grace had been impressed with the way the girl had carried herself. Now, these tears were fast beclouding all that she had thought perfectly clear.

She studied the sobbing young woman while she unconsciously brought forth a handkerchief which she offered to Elizabeth. It acted to bring the

obbing under control. Elizabeth sat up, mopping
t her eyes.

"I—I beg your pardon, Your Grace, for being so
illy in your presence. All of this is so unexpected,
ut this last has hurt me beyond bearing. Was it not
nough that my reputation was sullied beyond re-
lemption as soon as Tony deigned to notice me,
nust he lie to make my ruination more perfect?
urely what you are about to do to me now must
atisfy his hatred of me. Why does he go to such
lengths? Why does he despise me so? I have done
nothing to hurt him!" The outburst was too much
for her, and the tears streamed down her cheeks
again.

The duchess was plainly uncomfortable. Something was deucedly out of kilter, and she did not
like it one bit.

In a consoling fashion, she said: "I assure you,
my dear, it was not anything Tony said. We, all of
us, merely assumed that he-he—his reputation, you
know." A look of great irritation crossed her face.
"Oh, why did he have to leave us at this time!"

"He-he was here?"

"Yes. He knew you were coming! We all did!
Your con—Armbruster had foretold it. But that
was not good enough for him. He had to rush off to
London to find you—to face you with this—business. No doubt he'll return directly he finds you
gone."

"Oh then, please, Your Grace, have them take me away before he returns. I beg of you!" cried Elizabeth, rushing over to the duchess' chair and kneeling at her side, a pitiful look on her face.

"Stop that!" exclaimed Her Grace! "Stop it at once, child! What nonsense is this? You are supposed to plead *not* to be taken away. Do you know you are upsetting me? Now go back to your seat and behave yourself."

"Yes, Your Grace. I am sorry for my outburst, Your Grace."

Elizabeth resumed her seat, looking quite miserable.

Her Grace raised on admonishing finger. "Young lady, you are turning out to be a greater problem than I could have ever dreamed. Either you are a most consummate actress, or I have been led down the garden path about you. In either case, I cannot be happy about it. But this much I know, before ever you leave Oaklands, I shall have the truth of the matter.

"Now then, I will admit, had I met you under any other circumstances than these, I daresay I should have liked you. If it prove you are innocent of this crime, then I must admire you for the way you have stood up to it. I should have been petrified and could never have hidden it half so well. So much for that. I would have you at ease.

"It is possible that we have been hasty, but I

would have you understand that we have acted in accordance with what we know, and what we know is derived in the main from Harry Armbruster's story. Now I have no liking for the man or his oily tongue, but to the extent that his story jibes with Tony's knowledge of the situation, it appeared to make all the sense that was necessary, together with the fact that Armbruster not only predicted that you would come calling but pretty much what you would have to say. Now I take it, from what you have remarked, that appearances are deceiving and that you are completely innocent. Well, I would know wherein we were deceived."

"But, Your Grace, I never claimed to be *completely* innocent."

"Ah then, what do we waste our time for? If you are guilty, we can dispense with it all. Be a good child and go to Australia, won't you? You will cause us so much worry if you do not."

"But I am not guilty! I committed no crime!" protested Elizabeth.

The duchess sat up very straight in her chair. "My dear, you have chosen a most inopportune time to come to trouble us. We are giving a luncheon for our friends and acquaintances, this afternoon, and you must be disposed of before then. My husband will be quite out with me if I permit you to disrupt the gathering—oh dear, here he comes now!"

The duke's heavy tread was heard without. The

door swung open, revealing the large figure of His Grace. The expression on his face was a demanding one.

"What, Elvira, haven't you done with the baggage and sent her off to Australia yet?"

"No, Steven, I have not. I have run into a bit of difficulty, not the least of which is that she refuses to go."

"Nonsense, she's got to go! We can't send her to Newgate! The place is a filthy hole! I'd not send my worst enemy there! Hasn't she got any sense?"

Elizabeth gaped at him.

"She is bound she will not leave England."

"What has *she* to say to it! She's guilty and she knows it! Now she's got to pay the piper. She has no choice! She has got go to Australia—or else!"

Elizabeth was baffled. "Or else what, Your Grace? Only Newgate is left."

"Young lady, you are in trouble enough without adding insolence to your crimes. As I see it, you are guilty and have no choice in the matter."

"But I am not guilty, Your Grace. I—"

But the duke had wheeled upon his wife and exclaimed: "Elvira, what have you been doing in all this time? No wonder she will not consent to leave when you have not even convinced her of her guilt!"

"Your Grace, that is another little difficulty that has developed. Miss Brown *refuses* to acknowledge that she is guilty. I think it would be perfectly horrid of us to ship her off to Australia and she believing she was innocent. I am sure she would have a most dreadful time of it."

"Well, yes, that is true," agreed the duke, looking troubled for a moment. "Quite dreadful for her but, fortunately, that is not the case. There can be no doubt of her guilt and, what is more, she has got this lover fellow—Armbruster. He'll be seeing to her."

"Your Grace, I have no doubt that you can do what you will with me," Elizabeth said. "I cannot withstand you. But Armbruster is not my lover, and I am innocent of the crime!"

The duke glanced sternly at Her Grace.

She said: "I am very sure that the first part of what she claims is quite true, my lord—and if it is, so must be the rest."

Elizabeth looked at the duchess in surprise. It was so completely unexpected.

"What makes you think she and Armbruster—" began His Grace.

The duchess interrupted him. "Because she will not go to Australia, for one."

"That is no reason!"

"It is, indeed. The reason she will not go to Australia is because it would take her far from the man she loves."

Elizabeth gasped in wonder.

"Elvira, I have always prided myself upon the superior mental qualities of my wife. It disheartens me to see your intelligence fail you for once. You are saying that she wishes to go to Newgate because that is where her lover is. That, my dear, is a love beyond description and pure Banbury."

"Dear Steven, I have never claimed to be any cleverer than I need be and so I shall tell you I am not saying anything of the kind, only that the man she loves—not her lover in the sense you have used the term—the man she loves is in England, and she will stay here at any cost to herself."

"Does she expect the blighter to join her in Newgate, then?" asked the duke, quite baffled.

The duchess laughed merrily. "I hardly think *you* would allow it! He happens to be your own son!"

Elizabeth gasped. "I never said so!" she cried.

"Blast the boy! Are we in this scrape all because of his damn petticoat capers? You, girl, is this true?" he demanded of Elizabeth.

"Your Grace, I am sure I am far beneath my lord Montreat's notice. It was only a business arrangement I had with him."

"It seems to me that has an awfully familiar ring to it," remarked the duke.

"Miss Brown," said the duchess sternly, "you are being evasive. The point at issue is not the marquis' interest in you but yours in him."

"I assure you, Your Grace, I never said to you that I loved your son."

"I thought not!" exclaimed the duke. "Elvira, what is all this in aid of?"

"It is simply that if she does love Tony, then we have misjudged the entire business, and we must have another explanation for it. Now, Steven, do not interfere. Miss Brown is a very clever young lady, but I think I have come to know something of her in this little time. Miss Brown, I would ask you a simple question. If my lord Montreat were in Australia, would you then be willing to be cast into Newgate?"

Elizabeth glanced at the duchess and slowly shook her head as she turned her eyes to the floor.

The duchess raised her eyebrows in triumph and conferred a superior sort of smile on His Grace.

The duke looked puzzled. "Then can anyone tell me why Miss Brown stooped to this odious scheme?"

Her Grace smiled. "We shall come to that anon. For the moment, I am satisfied, very satisfied that it is not a hardened malefactor we have to deal with."

"Hmph!" snorted His Grace. "It's all Tony's fault! Damned young fool. Miss Brown, I pity you for having lost your heart to my son. He is not worth a decent woman's consideration, certainly not yours. I warn you, you have lost your heart in vain to a very rackety fellow indeed. For one thing, although you're pleasant enough to behold, you will never do for the Marquis of Montreat.

His taste, you know, runs to a more-stylish type of beauty. You are not flashy enough to catch his eye. But I should not be disconsolate if I were you. You will have lost nothing, for he is a fool. I will go so far as to say he is an idiot. Why just the other day what does this son of mine do but, all hot to see some young thing away out in Bath, he goes charging off, his mind not at all where it should be, and smashes himself up in a ditch. Result? He is put to bed with a banged-up shoulder. Gad! I tremble to think what he will do to himself if he should ever find himself truly in love."

He was eying Elizabeth all during this monologue and seemed satisfied at the great variety of expressions that crossed her face as she listened to him. The very last was of shocked pain.

She exclaimed: "Tony was hurt?" and she turned to Her Grace with a wild question in her eyes.

"It is all right, child. He is fully recovered. So that is what this is all about? I begin to see a pattern. Tony never told you about it, did he?"

Elizabeth shook her head, and the duchess nodded knowingly.

The duke looked from his wife to Elizabeth and back again. He said: "I see that you are satisfied this female is not to be punished. Very well, give her £50 and a lecture on the evils of bad company and send her off. We have guests coming, you know."

The duchess placed a hand on Elizabeth's arm

as she replied: "Really, Steven, I cannot do that. I fear Miss Brown must stay on until I have gained a complete understanding of this business. And, as if you did not know, this happens to be the very same young lady on whose account our darling son smashed himself up."

The duke looked shocked. "You don't say," and he came over to Elizabeth and bent down to peer into her face, his lorgnette completely neglected.

Elizabeth could see that his eyes were piercing and intelligent. His face peered into hers for but a moment, but she had the distinct feeling she was being weighed carefully.

He straightened up and remarked casually to his wife. "I say, Elvira, that damned fool may not be such a damned fool after all."

A noise of carriages rolling up the drive was heard.

"Our guests, Steven," said the duchess.

"Yes, I heard. Well, I think I shall have something to show them. Can you imagine the look on old Sefton's face when I present my son's mistress to him!" He went off into a gale of deep laughter.

"Steven Quarnell!" cried the duchess. "You will do no such thing! Aside from the complete lack of propriety in such a gesture, your son has denied it and so does Miss Brown!"

He looked at Elizabeth and winked. "Well, you'll admit it would liven up the affair, what?"

Elizabeth could not help but chuckle.

"Well, if she will not go to Australia, we have no choice but to bring her along to luncheon. Will you do me the honor, Miss Brown?" He held out his arm.

Elizabeth looked a question at Her Grace.

The duchess smiled as she arose. "I fear we shall have to wait until Tony returns before we can see an end to this business; but for now, I think His Grace has rendered some sort of verdict. Do you understand, my dear?"

Elizabeth smiled as she got to her feet. "No, Your Grace. I am quite bewildered, but I am not as frightened as I was."

"Oh, I say!" exclaimed the duke. "I hope I did not overdo it, Miss Brown. I admit I was trying to scare you into confessing, but no more than that."

Elizabeth was astounded that he should apologize.

There was a tinkle of laughter from the duchess as she saw the expression on Elizabeth's face. "My dear, my husband could not maintain his threatening posture against you. That is why he asked me to see what I could do with you. I had to determine who was bluffing whom."

"Well, young lady, do you intend to keep me waiting all day?" demanded His Grace gruffly.

"But, my lord, I am still accounted base in your eyes. I cannot join you before your guests."

"I do not see that there is any need for you to be so high in the instep with the Duke of Verndon. You did not look down your nose at an invitation to

Claridge's from the Marquis of Montreat. Well, let me assure you I am at least as good as he."

Elizabeth burst into delighted giggles as she took his arm.

༈

It was a very informal gathering, luncheon was. Service was from a buffet, and the guests wandered about or sat at little tables set out upon the spacious open portico, accessible through great french windows from the huge drawing room. Elizabeth, who had appetite for neither food nor attention, was just as glad. She could carry a plate and pretend to partake, and no one would notice that she was not eating. As to attention, that she received far in excess of what she would have preferred, and it was all the fault of the host.

The friends and acquaintances of the Duke and Duchess of Verndon were an exalted group of personages. Nothing less than the rank of earl in titles were present except for a sprinkling of younger guests, offspring of some of the peers present, with lesser titles of courtesy. It hardly need be pointed out that never in her life before had Elizabeth been in anything like such august company. She was overawed and felt very humble and out of place. The great frame of the duke might have

been a veritable obstruction to their noticing her if
she could have maintained herself behind him, but
he would not have it. With the greatest of ease and
cordiality, he toured the rooms with her on his arm,
introducing her to one and all as Miss Elizabeth
Brown of Bloomsbury, a dear friend of the family.
It was a little short of amazing how the old gentleman, who had her all confused with wenches and
baggages and "some young thing in Bath" not an
hour ago, now had not the slightest difficulty with
her name and direction.

Since he was bound to show her off to each and
every one of his guests—and his manner certainly
seemed to be quite puffed up as he went about it—
she put herself out to be as pleasant as she could. If
she hoped that her presence might be little noticed
and soon forgotten, she was in for great disappointment.

She overheard from one corner: "So that is *the*
Miss Brown!" and from another: "I'll wager there
is something very special about that one. Not in
Tony's usual style, y'know," and from another:
"Eccentric, perhaps. Dress doesn't do a thing for
her. Can easily afford better, don't y'know?"

And it went on for some hours, right on until
late afternoon when the guests began to depart.

Their Graces, keeping Elizabeth at their side,
bade them all farewell. After the last had gone,
Elizabeth began to make motions to depart too.

"Where do you think you are going, girl?" demanded His Grace.

"Why, since I will not go to Australia, and you will not send me to Newgate, I-I thought I might return home."

The duke placed a firm hand upon her shoulder, fixing her to the spot. "Not on your life, girl! You are staying right here until the marquis manages to find his way back to Oaklands. Knowing him, that could be months! But I have decided that you are *his* problem, and he will know what to do about you. By heaven, he'd better!"

"But, Your Grace, I may not be away for so long. My cousin Mary will be sick with worry over what has befallen me. She does not know where I am."

"And where is this cousin Mary of yours?"

"In Bloomsbury, of course, Your Grace."

"Why dammit, girl, that was not the least sensible in you!" he exclaimed. "How the devil is Tony to find you if your cousin can't tell him where you are—for that is where he went off to."

"I-I had no idea—"

"That's the trouble with you young folk. Never have any idea at all! Now there's Tony, bound to be chasing all over the countryside looking for you. Damned young fool'll probably wind up breaking his other shoulder."

"Oh, I pray to God he will not!" cried Elizabeth in alarm.

The big hand patted her shoulder comfortingly. "There, there, not to worry. He'll have learned his lesson the first time around. And next time, you be sensible, hear? Let Tony know where you're at! Can't spend his life chasing all over London after you, y'know."

"Cannot we send a messenger after him?"

"Ha! What's the sense of sending one fool after a bigger? Imagine what they'd have to say about it in the Lords. 'There's old Verndon chasing after that fool son of his again!' No, the answer to all our troubles with the lad is that he has got to settle down, get married and raise himself some brats, so he can have worries of his own. That'll keep him out of scrapes, that will! I say, you don't happen to know a proper female that'll bring him round to it, do you?"

"Steven, that will be quite enough!" admonished the duchess. "You are letting your sense of humor run away with you!"

Elizabeth chuckled.

The duke arched his eyebrows at her and turned to his wife. "Y'know, Elvira, this Miss Brown's idea of humor is almighty strange." He bent over to Elizabeth and asked: "Now what is it exactly that has tickled you so, m'dear?"

"I was just thinking that your son's sense of what is comical bears a striking resemblance to your own —and I did not find his funny at all!" she said, dryly.

"Did you hear her, Elvira? The girl laughs, but she does not think it funny. Oh, I tell you, Tony has got him a problem on his hands for sure!"

"Oh, go along with you, you odious fool!" exclaimed the duchess as, laughingly, she gave him a playful push.

The duke strolled away, chuckling to himself.

Elizabeth observed the look in the duchess' face as she watched her great husband depart, and it gave her a warm thrill within to witness it.

She asked: "Does His Grace always play at being a fool?"

"Not always, but when he appears to be most foolish, you can rely on it that he is not one at all."

"I thought, when he seemed to be so confused about me, he was, well, almost inane. I could not help laughing. I noticed that you did too, Your Grace."

Lady Elvira smiled. "Yes, he was doing it to a turn, and all for your benefit. He feared he had been unjust and too severe with you, that he had frightened you—"

"Indeed he had!"

"—when he had only meant to convince you that you had been found out. As you will learn, the Quarnells can be insufferably arrogant—"

"Tony is! Most decidedly!"

Her Grace smiled. "Yet you love him?" she inquired, as though there was no question about it.

"I have never said I did!"

"You do not have to. It is written all over you. You betray yourself so easily."

Elizabeth blushed. "I do not see how."

The duchess laughed lightly.

"Oh, my dear, just think back to how it was in the little study. The vilest accusations hurled at you elicited almost a placid resignation from you. You did not bewail your fate. You remained quite collected, and I thought you to be a most hardened sort of evildoer. But at the implication Tony had traduced you to us, that was a hurt to you beyond bearing and you wept bitterly. It told me all I needed to know. The business about your refusing to leave England could not have become clearer. I pressed you on it only so that my lord would understand that you could not have been a party with Armbruster."

"Your Grace, would you hate it very much if Tony were to—return my a-affection?"

Her Grace looked away and said: "His Grace is quite taken with you."

Elizabeth was surprised. "How could he be? He knows so little about me, and then there is this business to cast all manner of doubt—"

Lady Elvira patted her on her hand and interposed, blushing very charmingly: "My lord claims to have seen a look in your eyes that he has seen in mine." To hide her embarrassment, she took Elizabeth by the arm. "Come, child, and sit with me. Tell me your story from the beginning when you first met Tony. I want it in all detail."

"Oh, I could not, Your Grace! It would be too embarrassing!" Elizabeth exclaimed.

The duchess turned to her, a look of doubt in her eyes. "Did I not understand that there was nothing to embarrass you in your relations with my son?"

"My lady, it is not an embarrassment for me, but I am sure it must be for Tony."

"Oh," said the duchess, with a laugh of relief, "you refer to the encounter in your shop!"

"Great heavens! He did not tell you about *that!*"

"He had to, my dear, to protect your honor before us."

"Well, really, that is outside of enough! Must he crow about all his conquests?"

"You can hardly call that a conquest! Interestingly enough, you are the first, and only one, of his lady friends that my son has ever seen fit to discuss with us."

"That is no distinction I care for. Why—"

"Enough, Elizabeth! You will have plenty of opportunity to deliver your opinions on that subject to the culprit himself. Now, I would have you unravel all this mystery for me."

ॐ

And so it was that in the most natural way, Elizabeth found herself pouring out her tale, together with her most intimate thoughts to the mother of the man she loved—and a peeress to boot—and she had not the least reluctance to do so. Although Lady Elvira was the easiest person in the world to talk to, she was not the world's best listener. Not that she wasn't interested, but that she never hesitated to interrupt if anything was not made crystal clear to her. The fine features of her piquant face were very expressive of her intentness and also of her appreciation of what she was hearing. More than once, Elizabeth found herself blushing at some of Her Grace's more pithy comments.

Her narration flowed on quite effortlessly, from her first encounter with the marquis up to the point where she had declared, to Mary, her resignation to becoming another conquest of Tony's. At that point, the duchess remarked: "If that is how you felt, why behave so submissively? You should have accepted his offer and wed him."

"But you cannot be serious, Your Grace!" protested Elizabeth. "It was just another of his odious jests!"

"No, it was not. It may not have been a well-considered offer, but he did mean it. I suppose you could not be expected to realize it, but he'd never have brought you to Claridge's otherwise."

Elizabeth looked at my lady in doubt. "But he could not have meant it! He was piqued with me and would have his revenge. So I understood it and resolved that as long as he maintained a pretense of nterest, I would lead him a merry chase—and-and nake him pay for his pleasure."

The duchess laughed. "I am sure it would have come to exactly the same thing if, under those circumstances and feeling as you did, you married him —and I should not have been at all in sympathy with him."

"But he did not love me!"

Lady Elvira raised an eyebrow. "Probably so. It may explain why he was so wroth with Armbruster, when he claimed to have been your lover, that he knocked him down. And no doubt it was no feeling at all for you that made him dash off to London, in a rage, to find you."

"Well, if he could believe that of me, I don't care how angered he became!"

"Yes. Well, what happened next?"

Elizabeth picked up the thread of her story, but she was somewhat disturbed. It seemed to her that somewhere in the past month she had missed a turning and that she might never find her way back.

The next discussion came about toward the end, the point at which Elizabeth had finally located the documents.

"I feel such a fool now to have raised such a fuss over two worthless pieces of parchment," she remarked.

"What was in your mind regarding them at the time?"

"I hoped I could use them to destroy Tony!"

"What would that have gained you?"

"He never came to Bath! He never wrote to explain!"

"Well, now you know why he did not. He was thoroughly laid up."

"Still he could have written more than just that one cold little note! Or, if it was so much of an effort, could he not have added just a little something to your letter? Was that asking so much?"

"Yes, that was odd of him not to. I thought surely he had. He said he planned to as soon as he could use his hand more freely."

Elizabeth sniffed. "It could hardly have mattered to him. I guess I have been a silly fool throughout."

"Let me understand something. You were safely away from him at Gryfynskepe and believed that, given the opportunity, the marquis would have taken every advantage of you. Then what is all this about? Why should it have upset you? You were safe from him."

"I-I did not wish to be all that safe!"

Lady Elvira burst into merry laughter. "I thought as much!" She proceeded: "So feeling quite put out with him, you went on with this business with Armbruster."

"Why did he not write to me and let me know that he had been hurt?" asked Elizabeth rather plaintively.

"I daresay his pride would not allow it. He felt

ery foolish for having wrecked himself and his rig,
nd his father ragged at him unmercifully for his
apse. You have heard how my lord goes on about
he 'damned young fool'!"

"I am sure His Grace does not mean it the way it
ounds."

"Quite so. It is truly a term of endearment when
he uses it to refer to his son. So it begins to appear
hat your heart and hands were not clean when you
went to speak with Armbruster."

Elizabeth lowered her gaze. "Yes, my lady. But
hat was only part of it. I sought Armbruster out
as much to confirm my suspicion that he had some
part in the raid. And, too, I was not all that sure of
how the documents could be put to use against
Tony. I was sure he would know."

"I have no doubt that you were successful."

"Oh yes, I had no trouble at all on that score.
When I left, he had the impression that we should be
confederates and more, I daresay."

"It surprises me that he should have been so taken
in," remarked the duchess.

"Well, I flattered him a little and I set him down
a little and, after I had impressed him that I was not
so green, I pointed out that it was I who must discover the parchments and hold them. He would
have no chance to interfere, with Cowles now on
the alert and guarding me. Incidentally, my lady,
before they laid Cowles low, he had managed to
pretty well ruin Armbruster's people for him. They

lost their taste for the enterprise and decamped leaving Sir Harry with no alternative but to g along with me. I wanted you to know that—abou Cowles."

Lady Elvira's eyes narrowed. "You are making point, I think?"

"Your Grace, Cowles and my cousin Mary wil wish to marry, but he fears you may object."

"Why should I object? Cowles has my blessing in anything he wishes to do. I am sure he know it."

"Well then, it is Tony's approval he is doubtfu of."

The duchess appeared to think about that for moment. Then she nodded. "Yes, I think I under stand what Cowles is afraid of. I should say, my dear, that you had better get Tony in a good moo and then confront him with it."

"You think he may object?"

"I think you had best ask him. I'll not answer for Tony. Tell me, how much did you plan t extort from the Quarnells?"

"I never got so far in my thinking. I could no bear the idea that so loathsome a creature shoulc ever get the better of Tony."

"Oh, but it was all right for you to ruin him Just so long as no one else dared."

Elizabeth sighed. "It would have been so reward ing to have had the Marquis of Montreat humbled before me—but only for an instant, you understand

could not ever wish to see Tony anything other
than he is even though where I am concerned he
is blind."

"Sad, very sad, I must say. So you could not go
through with it. Still, you were in a position to ask
for something—a fee, say, a handsome fee for the
work you had done—yet you did not. Why?"

"I had thought to ask that I be forgiven my debts
in exchange for the documents but, as I had incurred them through my own folly, I could not in
good conscience make the request—especially as I
had contemplated betraying you all." She sighed.
"I don't think the Marshalsea is all that much
better than Newgate. I must owe close on to 2,000.
I could labor for a lifetime and never amass such
a sum."

"Surely it is not so much as that?"

"Aye, it is. Before I came out here, I received an
additional £700 from Cowles. I gave it to Mary as
a wedding gift. She might as well have some good
from it, and twelve hundred or twenty, it is all the
same to me."

"Have you been keeping an account?"

"But, of course! I am a woman of business!"

"That will come as a bit of a surprise to Tony.
But why did you allow yourself to become so over-
burdened with debt? That is hardly good business
practice."

"Tony insisted. I knew what he was up to but
feared that I should lose the commission and any

chance of seeing him again if I demurred. Necessary expenses, he claimed!"

"Amazing! A case of two noodles trying to entrap each other and finding only consternation for their pains! Well, it is late and dinner will be served soon. I hope you have a change of clothing."

"No, Your Grace, I came away from the inn without my luggage—not that I have anything more suitable than what I have on."

"It is not in the first style."

"I know, but I feared you would never think me an antiquarian if I made my appearance in some of the finery Tony made me buy."

"Well, I should say you have gone too far! You have more the appearance of an antique than an antiquarian. I would give you the freedom of my wardrobe, but not a thing would fit you. Well, we shall go into Sevenoaks, tomorrow, and see what we can have made up for you there. I know of a modiste of some talent. She can put something together that will do until I can get you to the shops in London."

"But, Your Grace, I have no money. I have barely enough to see me home, and it is not even mine. It is Tony's."

"Oh, I should not worry too much about it. I daresay we shall find some satisfactory way of settling your account, I think."

"It is such a terribly large sum," said Elizabeth
in awe as she thought about it.

"Yes, it is, but as His Grace will undoubtedly
point out—I can just hear him: 'I always say you'll
get nothing if you pay nothing. Now here's a matter of £2,000 and, for what we got, it was a bargain. I say it was well spent and I'll hear no more
about it!' and that will be that."

"I do not understand."

"You will, my dear. You will."

　　　　　　　　　　ॐ

The next morning, shortly after breakfast, Lady
Elvira and Elizabeth were standing in the great
vestibule discussing their forthcoming visit into
town. As His Grace had only been informed of
their plans at the breakfast table, he was now up in
his chambers, changing into something appropriate, having thoroughly blasted all females for never
making up their minds and telling him anything.
He was damned if they'd go without him.

As they waited for His Grace to finish upstairs
and join them, there came the rattle and jingle of
a carriage without. It came up fast and ground to a
stop. Seconds later, the front door was flung open,
and a tall, lithe young man in riding dress appeared

on the threshhold. There was not a hint of black
in anything he had on.

At his entrance, both woman looked up.

"Tony!!" cried Elizabeth joyously.

"Beth!!" cried Tony, his face showing the strain
of hard riding and worry. "What the devil are you
doing here, you little idiot? This is the last place
you should have come to!"

He strode over to her and placed a protecting
arm about her shoulders as he faced his mother.

"Your Grace, I don't care what she has done,
you shall not send her to Australia!"

The duchess calmly agreed. "Yes, my lord, it
would be far too difficult. She will not go."

My lord Montreat stood and glared down at the
little duchess. "Surely, Mother, you cannot dream
of sending her off to Newgate? I will never permit
it!"

"Nor will your father," said Her Grace, continuing very serenely.

"He won't?" asked Tony, looking nonplussed.
"Well, pray tell me exactly what you intend doing
with her."

"Really, Tony, your father does not see why we
should be troubled in this matter. She is really no
concern of ours. It was your property and your
money, so, in all justice, she is your problem. Do
you not agree?"

"Yes! Of course! No reason at all for you to be

roubled. Just leave her in my hands. I shall see to
t."

"Good, I am glad you are so agreeable. Pray tell
me exactly what you intend doing with her."

"Why-er-I shall see that she goes back to Blooms-
oury. Best place for her to be while I-er-give some
hought to it. I mean I cannot say right off what I
hall do, but I'll do something—"

"And where do you intend to do this thinking,
may I ask?"

"Oh well, I shall retire to London where I can
keep an eye on her, Your Grace. We would not
want her to slip away, you know."

"I cannot think that I should like that arrangement, Tony. She had best remain here while you do
your thinking. And, Tony . . ."

"Yes, Mother."

"When you come to offer another proposal, it
had better be a vast improvement over what you
now have in mind."

Tony smiled. He stepped to his mother, gently
swung her up and kissed her on the forehead. As
gently, he set her down and said, softly: "I had best
speak with my father."

"I think you had better," agreed the duchess as
he straightened out her clothing.

"You will not let her get away?"

The duchess placed a protective arm about Elizabeth's waist and gave her a little squeeze. "You may rely upon it."

Tony grinned. "Ah yes, I had better speak with Father."

"So you have said."

"How is your shoulder, Tony?" asked Elizabeth.

"Quite well, thank you. Oh, you have heard!"

"I have heard that you smashed yourself up rushing off to some wench in Bath."

"I see His Grace has been up to his old tricks again," said Tony, going very red about the ears.

"Why did you not write to tell me of your mishap? Nothing of this would have happened if you had!"

"What fine excuse is that! It certainly was not anything for me to brag about, but I do not see that my not informing you gave you license to consort with that foulmouthed Armbruster!"

"My lover?" asked Elizabeth, sweet to the point of nastiness.

Tony went to her and grabbed her by her shoulders. He gave her a little shake and scowled. "Don't you dare say that to me! He never was your lover! Not for one moment can you make me believe it! You used him just as you tried to use me!"

"And what if I did! Did you serve me any better trapping me into debt that I can never repay—or had you not some other sort of payment in mind?" she shot back at him.

The grip on her shoulders eased, and he smiled down into her face.

"So you knew what I was up to?"

Elizabeth smiled back at him. "I knew," she murmured.

His eyes narrowed suspiciously. "Yet you went right along with it? Have you any idea how much I spent on you?"

"To the last penny!"

He looked somewhat taken aback, and the duchess laughed.

Turning to his mother, he said: "Your Grace, methinks I detect your fine hand in all of this."

"My dear boy, do not deceive yourself. It seems that I am not the only female to take your measure. You cannot know how happy it makes me."

"Mother, tell me what I am to do with her."

"You might speak with your father. I am sure that he may have a suggestion or two for you."

"Yes, I certainly shall and right away. Where shall I find him?"

"He is up in his chambers getting ready. He is to squire us into town. Beth has got to have some clothes, for she cannot continue in that dreadful getup. She did not come prepared to stay and had no idea we should hold her—ah—prisoner."

"Hah! A fine prisoner she is with all the resources of the Quarnells about to be applied to her benefit. I daresay the situation in that regard will get worse as time passes and not better."

"Yes," replied Her Grace. "It certainly does begin to appear that way, does it not?"

Tony chuckled and went for the stairs two at a time.

Lady Elvira turned to Elizabeth and remarked: "I should say things are going quite well."

"I think he really loves me," said Elizabeth with wonder in her voice.

"Do you really!" said the duchess and laughed and laughed.

It was not more than a few minutes, and Tony came charging back down.

There was a determined look upon his face as he came over to Elizabeth and took her by the arm.

"Come!" he ordered her sternly. "We have things to discuss, you and I."

She permitted him to lead her away, and he took her into the little study she knew so well from her experience of yesterday.

"Must we talk here?" she asked. "I have no fond memories of this room."

"It will do. What I have to say to you should help to erase the memory of whatever unpleasantness you suffered yesterday. I must say you seem to have survived it all very well. I have an idea that you are not at all behind hand when it comes to